A great roar sounded
from the far end of the room.

The door began to open wider as a torch's golden glow fell on a tall figure with a long neck and tail.

"Do you see it?" Andrew whispered from his hiding place behind an upended table.

"I see it," Lian said softly.

The figure was a dinosaur, a Troodon, and it was wearing *armor!*

After it glanced around the room and left, the three friends rose from their hiding places.

"We all agree that there's no way out of here from this room, right?" asked Andrew.

Ned and Lian nodded.

"There's only one thing we can do now," said Lian. "We'll have to explore the city."

"Okay," said Andrew. "I guess the only question now is: How happy will that Troodon be to meet three uninvited guests?"

DINOTOPIA®
LOST CITY

by Scott Ciencin

BULLSEYE BOOKS

Random House 🏠 New York

To my beloved wife, Denise.
Words can't begin to express how much I love you.
Forever and always, my angel. And beyond.
Special thanks to Alice Alfonsi and Jim Thomas,
my amazing editors.
—S.C.

Very special thanks to
paleontologist Michael Brett-Surman, Ph.D.,
James Gurney, and Scott Usher.

A BULLSEYE BOOK PUBLISHED BY RANDOM HOUSE, INC.

Library of Congress Catalog Card Number: 94-44454

ISBN: 0-679-86983-2

RL: 5.5

Printed in the United States of America 10 9 8 7 6 5 4 3 2

Cover illustration by Michael Welply

LOST CITY

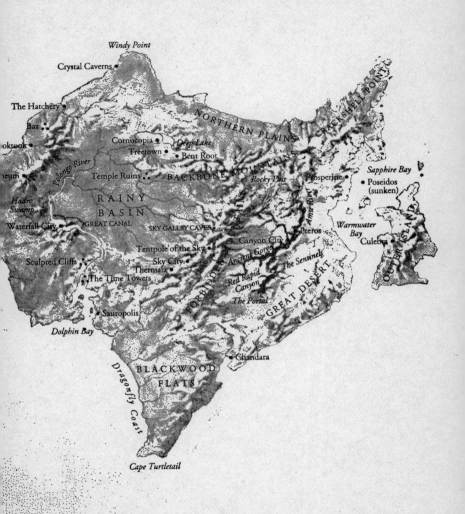

Windy Point

Crystal Caverns

The Hatchery

Baz

oktook

eum

Polongo River

NORTHERN PLAINS

Cornucopia

Deep Lake

Treetown

Bent Root

CROCKSHELL POINT

Temple Ruins

BACKBONE MOUNTAINS

Rocky Pass

Prosperine

Sapphire Bay

Poseidos
(sunken)

RAINY

Hadro
Swamp

BASIN

Amu Riv

Warmwater
Bay

Waterfall City

GREAT CANAL

SKY GALLEY CAVES

Pteros

Culebra

Canyon City

Tentpole of the Sky

Ancient Gorge

OUTER ISLAND

Sculpted Cliffs

Sky City

FORBIDDEN

The Sentinels

Thermala

The Time Towers

Red Rapid
Canyon

GREAT DESERT

Sauropolis

The Portal

Dolphin Bay

Dragonfly Coast

Chandara

BLACKWOOD

FLATS

Cape Turtletail

CHAPTER 1

Andrew Lawton sat thinking in the driver's perch of a large wagon. Just in front of Andrew was a fifteen-foot-tall dinosaur. The dinosaur hummed quietly to himself as he pulled the wagon forward with ease. His eyes remained fixed on a distant line of hills.

Night was closing in around Andrew and the dinosaur. Stars were beginning to appear in the darkening sky. The earth under the wagon's wheels took on an amber hue in the fading light.

Suddenly, Andrew sat up straight. "I've got one!" he said excitedly. "There was this family I spoke with. They were traveling through the Rainy Basin, and their child was lost—"

"You told me that one already," Thumptail said over his shoulder. A harness that looked a bit like an upside-down horseshoe was fitted over the Pachycephalosaurus's neck. Lines led back to the wagon. The dinosaur's rough skin was covered with soft green stripes. Thumptail's skull was a shiny pink dome surrounded by a circle of small spikes and horns.

Andrew was slight for his thirteen years. He had curly brown hair, doe eyes, and soft features. His loose-fitting lavender tunic was belted at the waist with a length of silver cloth. Baggy, deep-blue pants hung down to his sandals.

Andrew's brow furrowed. He tried to think of a tale he'd learned in the village today that he hadn't already told his friend on their journey home. "Did I mention the one about the man who ran into trouble because he was mistaken for someone else?" Andrew asked.

Thumptail nodded. "You did. That was rather amusing."

"What about the little Panoplosaurus who lost his parents and bonded with a crotchety Daspletosaurus? Their species were supposed to be natural enemies."

"That's an old story. Now the two species get along fine."

Andrew sighed. "Yes, I suppose it is an old story. But that Chingkankousaurus told it so well. You should have heard him. I want to make up fine stories like that."

"You already do, Andrew," Thumptail said.

"You think so?"

"Yes. You have a good imagination. You should enter one of the festivals of tales. I'm sure you'd win."

Andrew shook his head. "I don't think so," he said. "I'm not very good at winning competitions."

Thumptail was quiet for a moment. "Andrew,

2

what is it about storytelling that makes you happy?"

Andrew shrugged. "I don't know. I just need to do it. Even if no one is around, even if I can't get anyone to listen, I need to tell my stories."

Thumptail grunted. "Perhaps one day you will travel all over Dinotopia, delighting many with your tales. You could even tell the story of how Ned came to the island!"

Andrew smiled as he thought of his adopted older brother. Tall and handsome, Ned was easy with people and skilled in games. He was everything Andrew wished he could be.

"I remember when Ned first came to Dinotopia," Thumptail continued. "He learned our languages so quickly. And the notion of humans and Saurians living together seemed perfectly reasonable to him. Not like other Dolphinbacks, who take so much time to feel at home on the island. Do you remember what he said about his rescue? After the shipwreck?"

Andrew nodded. "That he didn't really need the dolphins' help to reach the island, but he didn't want to hurt their feelings."

"What a witty lad!"

The dinosaur hummed a song he had learned in the nearby city of Chipcharool. He tapped his heavy tail against the wagon in time with the song. Thumptail did this all the time; it was how he had earned his name.

"Andrew," said the dinosaur, "you know there is

going to be a storytelling event at this year's Dinosaur Olympics, don't you?"

"I heard something about it."

"Have you entered?"

"I might," Andrew said. He didn't want to admit how much the idea of entering the contest scared him.

Thumptail eyed Andrew over his shoulder. "You've competed in the Olympics before."

"Sure," said Andrew. "And I've always lost, too."

"Those were athletic competitions. This is story-telling!"

"I know, but—I'm not like Ned. He wins just about every competition he enters. I usually end up in last place. But that's okay. A person should know what he *can* do and what he *can't.*"

Thumptail sighed and turned back to the road.

Andrew laughed good-naturedly. "I'll think about it, okay? You know I love storytelling. I just don't know if I'm ready to do it in a competition."

Thumptail started humming again. Andrew smiled and looked up at the sky. It was almost completely dark. With a start, Andrew realized how late it was. They were running hours behind.

It was his own fault, he knew. Andrew worked at his father's inn in a small village called Grindstone. When he had a chance to visit the thriving city of Prosperine, he often got sidetracked. The people there were so interesting. What stories they had to tell!

Andrew was already getting ideas for another tale

of his own. He sighed. His father, who had once been an officer in the British navy, didn't completely understand Andrew's fascination with storytelling. And it wouldn't make a good excuse for being late—especially when Andrew was bringing back supplies for the upcoming Dinosaur Olympics. Joseph Lawton would have a dozen people waiting at the inn by now.

"Did you fall asleep?" Thumptail asked.

"What?" Andrew replied. "No. I was just thinking about how late we're going to be."

"Don't worry," Thumptail said. "I'm sure you'll come up with a reasonable excuse. If not, I'll smooth things over with your father."

Andrew gave the dinosaur a smile. "You're a good friend," he said. He looked around and took in the splendor of the countryside. Then something caught his eye.

What was that ridge in the distance? In the twilight it looked strange, almost unnatural. Could it be the lost city of Halcyon? Andrew knew that the ruins lay somewhere along this route. But he'd never noticed them before....

Andrew looked again at his friend. He was about to mention the strange rise when he saw a patch of darkness in the road just ahead. Thumptail was staring up at the stars, not watching the road. With a sudden feeling of dread, Andrew realized what the dark patch was.

Andrew jumped to his feet. "Thumptail, stop!" he

cried. "There's a—" But it was too late. Before Andrew could complete his warning, he watched his friend step right into a gaping hole in the road!

Thumptail cried out in surprise as his three-toed foot extended into empty space. Down and down his foot sank—three feet, four feet, six!—before connecting with solid earth. Off balance, Thumptail lurched to the side. The dinosaur howled in pain as he fell to the ground, all his massive weight crashing down on his trapped limb.

Andrew echoed his companion's scream as the harness between the dinosaur and the wagon pulled tight and the wagon began to capsize. Andrew was abruptly spilled onto the road, the wind knocked out of him. Gasping for breath, he saw a nightmarish shadow out of the corner of his eye. He looked up.

The wagon was falling on him!

CHAPTER 2

There was no time for Andrew to get to his feet. Quickly, he rolled away from the wagon until he heard the roaring weight strike the earth. A breeze rippled over him.

The edge of the wagon had missed him by inches!

Gasping for air, Andrew sat up. He crawled over to Thumptail. The dinosaur's head lolled in pain.

Andrew felt tears sting his eyes. He touched the side of the dinosaur's head and stroked the softness near his snout.

"I'm going to get help," Andrew said softly.

Thumptail nodded. His dark eyes gleamed with appreciation. "An—drew—" he said, gasping.

"I tried to warn you," Andrew said. "I'm sorry."

"Do not...be so hard...on yourself," Thumptail managed to say. "Breathe deep...seek peace....You are...good lad."

"Is there anything I can do?"

"Yes...watch where you're...going."

Andrew smiled. Rising unsteadily, he began to

walk. The trip home would take half the night. He wanted to run the entire way, but he knew he had to pace himself.

Not far into the journey, Andrew felt the first few drops of rain. He looked around for a shelter but saw none. Just as well, he thought. Thumptail needed his help. He'd lose time if he waited out the storm. A little rain wouldn't kill him.

As if in answer, a clap of thunder sounded, and the downpour began. Andrew trudged on through the freezing-cold rain.

After about ten minutes, the storm let up. Above the horizon, Andrew saw flashes of lightning. Clouds passed over the moon, and the way became difficult.

During one of the lightning flashes, Andrew saw that he had wandered off the road. Using the lightning to see, he found his way back and then continued on.

At a bend in the road, Andrew climbed a rise and saw what looked like a hooded and cloaked man in the distance.

"Sir!" Andrew cried. A rumble of thunder drowned out his words. The figure in the distance did not seem to notice him.

Though it meant leaving the road, Andrew walked in the stranger's direction. The figure stood on a slight hillock. Beyond him lay the jagged spires of the unnatural rise Andrew had noticed much earlier.

Was it the lost city? Andrew wondered. Perhaps the stranger would know.

He caught himself. All that mattered right now was that Thumptail was in pain. Perhaps this man would be able to help.

"Sir?" Andrew said as he got closer. "Sir, excuse me?"

The hooded figure stiffened, but did not turn.

Andrew continued, "My friend's been injured. He needs help. Is there anything you can do?"

The figure was close now...only a few feet away.

"Please," Andrew said.

The stranger hung his head low and took a step away from Andrew. Something made the boy uneasy, but he couldn't let the man leave.

"Wait!" Andrew called, grasping the figure's shoulder. What Andrew felt beneath the rough cloth was odd. It was not the soft yielding flesh of a man. Instead it was hard and spiky. Segmented.

Lightning flashed overhead. The stranger turned. The harsh light framed the cloaked figure for a single moment. It was a dinosaur of some sort. The jaws were longer than Andrew's forearm and filled with sharp teeth. The snout was sharklike. The eyes were golden with catlike slits.

That alone would not have been enough to unnerve Andrew. What filled Andrew's heart with terror was what he saw when the dinosaur's cloak fell open.

The dinosaur wore armor and carried weapons! Andrew saw a sword in a scabbard and some kind of ax. Everyone on Dinotopia understood that weapons were enemies even to their owners. To see a dinosaur

9

or human dressed this way on Dinotopia was unthinkable—yet here it was!

There was something else, too. In this dinosaur's blazing eyes Andrew saw a savage anger. Was this a meat-eating dinosaur from the Rainy Basin? What was he doing here? How had he found armor and weapons?

More important, would he harm Andrew?

The dinosaur raised his clawlike hand. He looked as if he were reaching for his sword!

Andrew screamed. The dinosaur bellowed fiercely. Andrew spun and raced back toward the road. He heard sounds behind him. The dinosaur was surely following!

Andrew ran and ran. He came to the road and followed its course, praying he would encounter other humans. Or friendlier dinosaurs!

Finally, his foot stepped upon a sliding rock, and he fell down. Gritting his teeth, Andrew turned and looked up. He expected to see the dinosaur towering over him, sword drawn. Instead there was nothing. Andrew was alone.

Scrambling to his feet, Andrew looked around and saw a figure in the far distance—the cloaked dinosaur. He had run in the other direction! Andrew could see him on the other side of the valley, racing toward what must surely be the lost city.

Had that fierce-looking dinosaur been frightened of him? Why?

The entire way home Andrew puzzled over the odd encounter. He'd been looking for new and exciting stories, he thought to himself, and now he had found one.

CHAPTER 3

Andrew burst into the taproom of the Dragon's Snout Inn. He was out of breath and covered in sweat. Though he had felt close to collapsing only moments earlier, the sight of his home had filled him with renewed energy.

The inn was dark. Less than a dozen people sat near the taproom's fire. They looked up as one.

"Father!" Andrew called to a wild-haired, barrel-chested man.

Joseph Lawton regarded his son with concern. He wore a Cheshire frock, brown leggings, and black boots. His face was covered in tiny scars and a thick beard. Katya, Andrew's mother, sat beside him. She wore a violet dress that Lian, one of Andrew's friends, had made for her. Her dark hair and pretty green eyes seemed to shine in the firelight.

"It's Thumptail! He's hurt!"

Andrew's father sprang to his feet. Ned suddenly appeared at his side. Andrew related the details of the accident. He didn't mention his bizarre encounter on the road. It hardly seemed important compared to getting help for his friend.

Joseph turned to Ned and immediately rattled off a series of instructions. A Shantungosaurus who lived nearby would have to be wakened and a cart large enough to hold Thumptail found. Ned immediately sent one of the Saurians gathered at the inn to find the Shantungosaurus. Then Ned began to make inquiries about the cart.

Andrew watched Ned, amazed at the way his adopted brother stayed so calm during the crisis. Joseph gestured to his friends. They all jumped from their seats and followed him to the door. As Joseph passed his son he reached out and mussed the lad's hair. "Get into some dry clothes, Andrew. I don't want you sick. It'd worry your mother half to death."

"But not you?" Andrew asked.

"You're a Lawton!" the man said. "We're a tough breed. Just humor me." He smiled.

"Yes, Father," Andrew said with a grin.

In a few minutes, Andrew had changed clothes. He returned to the taproom to warm himself by the fire before joining the others. His hair was still damp.

Suddenly, a loud sniffing sound came from the doorway. "Do I smell a drowned water rat?"

Andrew's smile broadened as he turned to see Lian come in. A pretty girl with raven's hair and emerald eyes like Andrew's mother's, Lian had a grin that betrayed a fun-loving, adventurous spirit.

She wore a shiny crimson outfit with a large belt. Her black boots reached up to her knees. Andrew had teased her that she looked like a pirate whenever she wore this outfit. It only made her want to wear it as much as possible.

For the past two years, Lian had seemed very happy in Dinotopia, but every now and then a strange sadness would come into her eyes. It would never last long. Andrew guessed that she was missing her home and family in China.

What else could it be?

"Hi, Lian," Andrew said.

"Hi, yourself," Lian responded. "You look upset. Are you all right?"

"Worried about Thumptail."

Lian studied Andrew's tense features for a moment. "Um-hmmm?"

"What?"

"There's something else. I know you."

With a sigh, Andrew relented and told Lian about the hooded figure on the road.

"Why didn't you tell anyone else about this?" Lian asked.

Andrew shrugged. "I don't know. I guess I was afraid no one would believe me."

"Why?" Lian asked, surprised.

"Well, you've got to admit, it does sound pretty far-fetched. A dinosaur in armor, carrying weapons? Why not a man with wings? Or a tree that came alive and did a little jig? Most people wouldn't take something like that too seriously. Especially coming from me, someone who's always telling stories."

"You're being too hard on yourself. If you said you really saw this, people would believe you."

"Do you believe me?"

"Yes," Lian said. "But maybe you were right not to mention anything. Everyone's already worried over poor Thumptail. Let's not panic them."

Andrew swallowed hard. "Lian, what if there are more of those hooded Saurians, and they attack our caravan?"

"He ran away, didn't he?" Lian said. "It sounds as if you scared him as much as he scared you!"

"I hope you're right," said Andrew, thinking about the savage ferocity in the dinosaur's eyes. And those weapons! "I just wish we knew for sure...."

"We'll have the Shantungosaurus with us. He's fifty feet long. I think we'll be safe." She saw that Andrew wasn't entirely convinced. She raised a single eyebrow. "You're my friend, and you know I care about you, but sometimes I think you're a little over-dramatic."

"Sorry. Just comes naturally, I guess."

Lian put her hands on her hips and gave Andrew a little grin. "There's someone I think you should see," she said. "Come on."

Lian took Andrew's hand and led him upstairs to a small library. Inside, a robed dinosaur was studying a scroll on a reading machine. The Troodon, also known as a Stenonychosaurus, stood on a treadmill connected to a podium. The scroll was loaded into the viewing window in the podium. By taking a step or two, the dinosaur could pull down the scroll and continue reading.

Andrew drew back when he saw the dinosaur. For a brief moment, he thought he was looking at the hooded dinosaur he'd met on the road. The dinosaur reading the scroll had the same large eyes and tooth-filled snout.

Without disturbing him, Andrew and Lian went downstairs again.

"That's Malik the Timekeeper from Waterfall City," Lian said. "He stopped off here to visit friends before going on to the Dinosaur Olympics."

"Oh," said Andrew.

"He's as peace-loving a Troodon as you'll ever meet. The dinosaur you saw on the road—did he look like Malik?"

"Yes," said Andrew. "Except for what scared me—the armor and the weapons."

"Are you sure the Troodon you saw wore armor and not just some shiny jewelry?"

"Um—"

"That sword…could it have been a walking stick?"

"Well…"

"And what you took for an ax might have been some kind of tool for climbing, right?"

"I suppose."

"So," Lian said. "Are you sure you didn't overreact just a little?"

Andrew rubbed his head. "Well, when you put it that way, I guess I *was* pretty shook up. And with the lightning and all, it was hard to see."

Andrew and Lian turned as Ned appeared in the doorway. The older boy's features were bold and strong. His dark vest had been handmade by Andrew's mother. The powder-blue shirt and leggings he wore had been a gift from Andrew's father.

"There you are!" Ned said brightly. "We need you, Andrew."

"Really?" asked Andrew.

The older boy nodded. "We've got a long ride ahead of us. People are upset. They need you to entertain them with some stories. It will help take their minds off of Thumptail. Come on, we're just about to leave."

Ned turned and hurried off.

Lian smiled and put her hand on Andrew's back.

Andrew asked, "Do you think I should tell Ned?"

"If you want to," Lian said. "I'm sure he won't say anything if that's what you want."

"I don't know. I'm feeling kind of silly about the whole thing now."

They went outside and joined the caravan. Andrew rode in the cart that would be used to pull Thumptail. More than a dozen other humans and Saurians were with him.

Andrew told many of the stories he had heard in

17

Prosperine that day. He wove his tales with such enthusiasm that his companions managed to forget their troubles for a time.

Finally, Andrew tried an experiment. He told the group about his encounter with the cloaked figure, but he made it clear that it was just another of his stories. Andrew wanted to see how his neighbors would react.

"I—I came up to it," Andrew said. "It turned, and in the lightning I could see its face. Good people, it looked like one of the meat eaters from the Rainy Basin—wearing armor and carrying a sword! Before I could say anything, it let out a scream that just about scared me out of my skin!"

There was a collective gasp.

"You know," Andrew said, "there's always the chance that I really did see this dinosaur...."

"Oh, sure! And I saw a unicorn!" said Glover, an Othnielia. Nibbling on a vast garden salad he carried with him in a bowl, Glover looked very much like a scaly, oversized rabbit. He had a brown hide and a tan underbelly. "Remember the day Andrew said he saw a unicorn? Really had us going on that one! What a clever and playful boy!"

"I remember about the unicorn," said another Saurian. "Andrew talked one of us into wearing a horn just so Lian could see what one would look like. That was sweet!"

Raising an eyebrow, Joseph turned to face his

friends. "I rather like this new story so far. Mysterious and dark, true, but not all tales can be bright and fluffy. What say the rest of you?"

Several others agreed. A ten-year-old boy with straight black hair and brown saucerlike eyes said, "I like the stories where you can fly. Tell one of those!"

A plump woman in a blue frock said, "No, I prefer the one where lightning struck him as a child, giving him his curly hair."

Andrew's mother winked at him and blew him a gentle kiss.

A gaunt, sour-looking gentleman leaned back. "I'm sorry, young Andrew. I prefer your tale about the lad who had to chase his shadow from one end of the earth to the other. This story is not as thrilling."

"I guess you've got a point," said Andrew. "Who could believe a story like that, right?"

The humans and Saurians laughed. Troodons in armor, carrying weapons. Really!

Andrew looked at Lian. She smiled at him sympathetically.

Ned caught the secretive exchange, but said nothing.

CHAPTER 4

The sun was high by the time the rescue team managed to extract Thumptail from the sinkhole. The dinosaur roared with pain as his leg was eased out of its trap. He was loaded onto a cart pulled by a much larger dinosaur. The Shantungosaurus was more than fifty feet long. It was heavy and squat, with a short neck. Alternating splotches of lime and forest green covered its body.

Andrew stayed with Thumptail while other members of the rescue party set and bandaged his leg. To keep his mind off the pain, Andrew told Thumptail a story about the hare and the stars.

"So we have three little animals who are really good friends," Andrew said. "A hare, an otter, and a jackal. They find out that the humans have a wise custom: One day out of every month, the people go around the city and share their food with any who are hungry."

"This is a nice story," Thumptail said. The dinosaur's pain was still great, but he was relieved to be off the road and out of the ditch.

"The three animal friends decide that if people can do it, they can too. They each hoard food, then go in search of the needy."

"These are good little animals."

"Yes, they are," Andrew said.

Thumptail yawned. "I'm sorry. How rude."

"No, it's good," Andrew said, stroking the side of the dinosaur's face.

"Rub my head?" Thumptail asked.

"Sure," Andrew said. The dinosaur cooed with relief. Andrew continued the story, explaining that the otter found fish. The jackal went into town and scavenged through garbage for meat.

"Meat eaters," Thumptail said. "Blech."

Andrew laughed. "It's another culture."

"If you say."

"This is really the hare's story. He collects up a bunch of grass and carries it with him. But when he finds someone who is hungry, he realizes his mistake. Humans don't eat grass. He's sworn to provide a meal for a hungry person, yet he has nothing to give. Nothing except himself. Humans, you see, love to eat the flesh of the hare."

"Barbaric!"

"True. But—"

"You're not going to have someone eat the little bunny, are you?"

"Don't worry, don't worry. Let me tell the story, all right?"

Thumptail grunted cautiously.

21

"Anyway, the hungry old man laughs at the idea that this animal would give up its life to help him. So few humans would do the same."

"That's not how things are on Dinotopia," Thumptail said proudly.

"I know, but there are a lot of places in the world that don't know our ways. Now, do you want the rest of the story or not?"

Thumptail yawned again. "Uh-huh."

"The old man reminds the hare that it is forbidden on this special day for men to kill animals. The hare tells the old man to build a fire. When it is good and hot, the hare leaps in!"

"Oh, no!"

"Don't worry, he isn't hurt. For some reason, the hare doesn't burn. The little rabbit wonders how this is possible. It turns out that the old man is a wandering spirit. This spirit is so moved by the hare's willingness to sacrifice itself for others that it casts an image of the hare into the night stars. That way, the hare's courage and love, so much brighter than anything the spirit has seen before, will never be forgotten. That's it."

Thumptail was having trouble keeping his eyes open. "Did you make that one up?"

"No, I just heard it somewhere. Now sleep."

"Had to hear the…end of it." Then Thumptail whispered, "There are no…bunnies in the stars. Make it…a bear…next time."

With that, Thumptail drifted off to sleep.

Andrew smiled. He knew he had lessened his friend's pain a little. The story, as it had first been told to him, actually involved a hare and the moon. It was one of the first stories that led to the legend of the man in the moon. Andrew had changed it to the stars for effect.

Someone behind Andrew cleared his throat. Andrew started. He turned and saw Ned.

"See? I told you we needed you," Ned said with a grin. "You did a good job calming everyone down, especially Thumptail."

Andrew smiled. "Thanks."

"Hey, have you thought any more about the story-telling competition since we talked about it last?"

Andrew studied his shoes. "No," he said.

The older boy smiled. "Let me tell you something my daddy back in Louisiana taught me. Daddy always said, 'You got two choices in life. You can wait for lightning to strike you—or you can go look for a storm!' You see, Andrew? Lian and I are leaving for the Dinosaur Olympics tomorrow. We'd like you to come with us."

"I—"

"Just think about it. That's all you have to promise me for now. Square?"

"Square" was Ned's shorthand for "fair and square" or "is that okay with you?"

Andrew shrugged. "Okay. I'll think about it."

The rescue party was finishing with Thumptail's leg, and someone called to Ned. Thinking about what Ned had said, Andrew wandered off in the other direction. He walked and walked through the grass and trees until he realized he'd left the entire rescue party behind.

Though he had no particular destination in mind, Andrew soon found himself staring at the hillock where he had encountered the strange hooded creature. He suddenly felt drawn to it.

Go back there? he thought. What good would that do? What would it prove?

His feet ached from all the walking, so he sat at the side of the dirt road and took off his sandals. As he massaged his feet, he noticed that his footprints were clearly visible in the road. Looking more closely, he could see the tracks left from the rescue party this morning along with what seemed to be his footprints from the previous night.

Was it possible that the hooded dinosaur had left tracks behind too?

His discomfort already forgotten, Andrew eased his sandals on again and walked to the hillock. He was careful not to disturb any evidence. After a few moments, Andrew found his own tracks leading to the hillock, then the tracks leading away. The tracks leading away were deeper.

That didn't surprise him. He had run away in terror.

Andrew walked a little farther and gasped as he discovered the tracks left by the hooded figure. The dinosaur had three toes, that much was clear. But the second toe left a mark more in keeping with a claw. A deep divot had been dug where each of the second toeprints should have been.

Definitely a Troodon. Like Malik, Andrew thought.

Andrew followed the dinosaur's trail into the valley and across a wide field. As he climbed out of the valley he noticed a rock formation in the distance. It was gray and white, with streaks of yellow and pink. With a start, Andrew realized it was the unusual rise he'd noticed from the road the day before!

The longer Andrew stared at it, the more certain he was that he was looking at spires and towers. This was not a natural rock formation.

It was Halcyon. The lost city.

Andrew ran toward it, laughing with excitement. How many times had he been on the road from Grindstone to Prosperine and gone right past it without paying any attention? The lost city had been here all that time!

All Andrew knew about Halcyon was that it had been a walled city built out of the side of a mountain. People said a natural disaster of some sort had destroyed it.

Now Andrew examined the walls of a city that seemed to grow from stone. Erosion and decay had cracked the surface. The city's spires and globes were chipped and sunken. They looked half-formed. As far as Andrew could tell, there wasn't any way into the city. All the entrances had collapsed and filled with rubble.

Andrew walked around the city's half-buried main gates for several minutes before noticing a gap in the stone wall a hundred feet above. The gap was almost perfectly square. It had to be a window, decided Andrew. With the right equipment, someone could scale the walls and enter what had been Halcyon. What a story that would make!

A glint of light caught Andrew's attention. He turned and saw something lying in the dirt. It was near the base of the wall, almost directly beneath the window. Crouching, Andrew picked it up. The boy's jaw fell open. It was an armlet—a chunk of metal designed to wrap around the arm of a warrior. Part of a suit of armor, perhaps.

Armor? Warriors?

He hadn't been seeing things after all!

But there had been no warfare on Dinotopia for a very long time. Centuries? Millennia? Andrew wasn't sure. Such things had never interested him. Violence was not the stuff of his tales.

He stared at the armlet. How had this relic remained unaffected by the elements for so long? It should have been rusted through. Instead, it was shiny and bright. Intricate patterns were carved into the armlet, designs unlike anything Andrew had ever seen. Was it some kind of writing? Perhaps it was a language that had been lost when Halcyon fell?

Andrew looked up at the window. Someone had cut that opening recently, Andrew thought. It was too perfectly square and unweathered to be as old as the rest of the walls. Whoever had made the opening had dropped this armlet. Thieves, perhaps.

Or strangers fond of cloaks and hoods.

"Andrew Lawton!" a voice hollered. "Where are you?"

Andrew looked up. One of his father's friends had been sent to find him. Rolling up his sleeve, Andrew slipped on the armlet. Then he rolled the sleeve down and ran back in the direction of the road. He never noticed the tiny flickers of light that came from the window above.

Or the eyes that followed his every move.

CHAPTER 5

That night, Andrew went looking for Lian. She roomed with a Leptoceratops named Henna, a golden-skinned dinosaur with a small horned face.

Henna let Andrew into her home. Lian's room was an addition around back. It had once served as a work area for Henna's late husband, so it was very large.

Outside Lian's room was a small plot of barren earth. After he'd first met Lian, Andrew had learned the importance of gardens to many Chinese people. He'd asked Lian why she hadn't made herself a garden.

"I am not worthy of a garden," Lian had said flatly.

Andrew had never brought up the subject again.

The door to Lian's room was open. Henna patted Andrew's shoulder and said she had work to do. She left the boy alone.

Andrew went to the doorway. Before he could call Lian's name, he heard her moving about inside.

"Come in!" she said.

Lian was on the floor, performing an exercise to loosen her muscles. She wore an outfit he'd never seen before: black slacks and a matching tunic with traditional yin and yang symbols embroidered on the right breast and the left sleeve. Various symbols of peace and serenity from Dinotopia had also been sewn onto the outfit.

Andrew looked around the rest of Lian's room. As far as he knew, only the eight small statues that sat on a ledge in the corner and a strange musical instrument had been salvaged from the shipwreck that had brought Lian to Dinotopia. A large beautiful rug woven by Henna hung upon the far wall.

"I can come back," he said, worried that he was interrupting her.

"Don't be silly," she said. "Why did you come by? To play Go?" Lian gestured toward a board with small black and white tokens. It was a replica of a strategy game from her native country. She had taught the Dinotopians to play. The Saurians had made up their own version called Tooth and Nail.

"No," said Andrew. "It's that hooded dinosaur I saw. I've got another story to tell...."

Andrew quickly told her of his journey to the lost city. Rolling up his sleeve, he took off the armlet and handed it to her.

"Don't you see?" he said. "The dinosaur I met on the road must have dropped this. Maybe he's in Halcyon!"

"Maybe...or maybe this came from someone else," Lian said, staring at the armlet and its strange designs.

29

"I want to try to get inside the lost city. It shouldn't be too hard. You have your climbing gear for that event you entered in the Olympics. We'll have a great time!"

"We?" asked Lian.

"Well…"

Lian looked up and handed the armlet back to Andrew.

"I was thinking the two of us," said Andrew. "Maybe Ned, too."

"What about your parents? And Henna?"

"I think they'd spoil the fun if they tagged along."

Lian frowned at him. "You know what I mean."

Andrew shrugged. "I've got it all planned out. I'll come with you and Ned tomorrow."

"To the Dinosaur Olympics?"

Andrew nodded. "Wagons come along twice a week to take people across the island. We'll tell our parents we've gone to meet one of those to take us to the Olympics. We'll leave a couple of hours early and take a look at the lost city. If it doesn't work out, we'll go back and meet the wagon. If we're having fun, we can catch the next wagon in a few days. No one will think twice about our being gone; no one will worry."

"Aren't you scared of running into that dinosaur with the sword?" asked Lian.

"Kind of," Andrew said. "But I figure we'll be careful not to draw attention to ourselves. We'll just see what's going on, then get out again. Besides, as you said, he didn't do anything to me. I was just startled."

"Uh-huh."

"I was."

She grinned. "I believe you."

"So you'll do it?" Andrew asked.

"I don't know," Lian said. "What makes you think I'd be interested? It sounds risky."

Andrew looked at her sideways. "You love taking risks."

"I do?"

"Sure," Andrew said. "Besides, you went to Skybax Camp. I know you learned lots of useful stuff there. And you're a really good climber."

Lian leaned in close. "What do you think we'd find there?"

"Something to tell stories about."

"You already tell wonderful stories."

Andrew frowned. "Most of my stories I heard from someone else or read. I want a story that's all mine, from something I discovered. I would love to tell a tale of adventure and danger. Of secrets and mysteries—you know, scary things."

Lian grinned. "Yes, your mother was telling me a story like that."

"She was?" Andrew said.

"Um-hmmm. She was collecting your laundry and telling me how frightening it was."

"Lian!"

"All right," Lian said, laughing.

"So will you go with me?"

"Yes."

"Really?" Lian had given in far too easily. "Wait a minute. You have your own reasons, don't you?"

A sudden fire came into Lian's eyes. "Andrew, there's something I want to show you. But you have to promise to keep an open mind."

"All right."

Lian went to her dresser, opened a drawer, and removed several dozen candles. With Andrew's help, she positioned the candles throughout the room and lit them. Then she knelt before her bed and drew out a long, plain wooden box. She reached into her sleeve and drew out a key.

"Remember that part about having an open mind?" asked Lian.

Andrew nodded.

"Go close the door. What I'm going to show you is very private."

He went to the door and closed it.

"Now stay like that. Don't turn around," said Lian.

"Okay," he replied, staring at the closed door. "You're not going to turn into salt or anything, are you?"

Behind him, he heard a lock click and the lid of the box come open.

"Excuse me?" asked Lian.

"A story I know. About a man named Lot."

Lian began moving what little furniture she had. The bed went up against the wall. Her low stools were next, then the box.

"Don't know that story," said Lian.

"I'll tell it to you sometime. It's about trust. And patience."

Lian was silent. Andrew heard the rustling of cloth, then a *whooosh* as something cut through air, like the wing of a Skybax.

What was she doing?

"Can I look now?" asked Andrew.

"No. You have to promise me something first."

"What's that?"

"When I say you can look, that's all you can do. No more talking. Not until I'm done."

"Done with what?"

"You'll see. I'll tell you when it's all right to talk."

Burning up with curiosity, Andrew agreed.

"And you have to promise, really promise, to keep an open mind."

"That's two somethings."

"Promise."

"Okay, okay."

He waited for several long seconds.

Finally, she said, "Now."

CHAPTER 6

Andrew turned and gasped at the sight before him: Lian held a sword! A sword!

Memories of his encounter on the road flooded back to him. He remembered his fear at the sight of the dinosaur's weapon. Had the creature lost its sword? Had Lian gone back and found it?

Andrew knew Lian would never hurt him or anyone else on the island. He just hoped she wouldn't hurt herself.

Lian stood with her back to Andrew, the sword in a two-handed grip. The sword's surface gleamed in the candlelight. Lian stared up at the sky through an opening cut into the ceiling. Directly below the opening, at Lian's feet, was a small pool filled with shimmering water. Lian had explained that almost every Chinese dwelling had such an opening in the ceiling and a pool beneath it to catch rainwater. It was called the Well of Heaven.

Suddenly, Lian burst into motion.

"Hai!" she cried. Her sword flashed, and two can-

dles were extinguished at once. Andrew had to bite his lip to keep from shouting in amazement. Lian had spun the sword so fast he'd barely seen it!

Lian whipped her sword over her head in a fluid circular motion and leaped into the air. Spinning, she lashed out with the sword again. Her feet barely touched the ground as she struck out half a dozen more candles. One snapped in half, sending its flaming head into the waters of the pool. It hissed as it struck. The room grew darker.

"Hai!" Lian cried again as she flashed the sword over her head, slicing apart another candle hanging from the ceiling. She danced around the room, lunging and retreating, slicing the air. One by one the candles flickered and faded.

For a moment, Lian was still. Then she rushed forward, spinning, turning, striking in all directions, her sword just a blur. Once, twice, three times. Darkness fell upon the room. It was eerie and beautiful. Only a few candles remained. Finally, Lian sheathed her sword. She walked over to the eight tiny statues and said a quick prayer.

At last, she said, "It's all right to talk, Andrew."

Andrew let out a long breath. "That was amazing! What you just did, I mean. Although it was kind of scary at first. I've never actually seen someone with a sword. Except for that dinosaur on the road—"

Lian suddenly interrupted. "I wanted you to understand that just because that dinosaur carried a sword didn't mean he was evil or dangerous. I own a sword, and I don't go around attacking people."

"Oh," Andrew said softly. "Did I insult you when I said how much the dinosaur's sword scared me?"

Lian laughed. "No."

"Where'd you get a sword, anyway?"

Lian went to the corner of the room, where the wood box waited, and she set the sword inside it. Then she closed the box and locked it. "I inherited it from my uncle."

Andrew looked at the box with Lian's sword. "I was taught that weapons are enemies, even to their owners. That's what everyone on Dinotopia believes."

Lian nodded. "I know. And I don't disagree with the idea. That's why I tell very few people that I have my uncle's sword. And that's why I keep it locked up. I don't want someone getting curious and hurting himself or someone else by accident."

"Why not just get rid of it, then?"

Lian sighed heavily.

"Sorry," Andrew said. "I guess that wasn't very open-minded of me, huh?"

"My uncle taught me that a warrior's sword carries a part of the warrior's spirit within it. So it's very special to me. I continue the exercises he taught me to honor his memory."

Andrew nodded. He still felt uncomfortable with the idea that his friend owned a weapon, but he could understand the spiritual meaning it held for her. And she *did* keep it locked away.

"Your uncle must have meant a lot to you."

Lian turned to face her friend. "He trained me in secret to become a warrior."

"In secret? Why?" Andrew asked.

"In my homeland, women don't become warriors. They cook and clean and look after children."

Andrew shrugged. "There's nothing wrong with those things. We all do that here."

"Yes," Lian agreed. She shook her head. "The irony is that I can be anything I want here. Anything *except* a warrior."

Suddenly, Lian laughed. "I know what my uncle would have said about my performance tonight. *'Inexcusable!'*"

Andrew frowned. "But you were incredible!"

"No," Lian said. "A good warrior is supposed to blow out the candles with the breeze from her sword. I never should have touched the candles. I left four candles lit. And two I cut in half."

"It was probably because I was here. I distracted you. Besides, you're not a warrior. Warriors fight and die. They hurt people."

"They defend. They honor their masters."

"In Dinotopia, you're your own master."

Lian shook her head. "There's no way you can understand. I can't help but wonder if there are people or dinosaurs in the lost city who might be more like me. Maybe they would understand."

Andrew smiled. "Well, there's only one way to find out."

CHAPTER 7

Morning had arrived, bringing with it a sweltering wave of heat. Andrew, Ned, and Lian had left hours earlier and were now trudging down the road to Prosperine.

"Having fun?" asked Ned.

"Loads!" answered Andrew, the sweat pouring into his eyes. Actually, he was. The three travelers carried heavy supply packs and the sun was hot, but these discomforts seemed insignificant. They were on their way to explore the lost city!

On the long walk, Andrew had told Ned about the lost city and his plan to investigate it. Ned agreed to come along—provided Andrew was in charge. The older boy thought it would be nice to have someone else giving the orders for a change. Andrew had been reluctant to accept the position as expedition leader, but Ned insisted. Andrew never saw the quick wink the older boy gave Lian.

Lian smiled broadly and sang a song that Ned had taught her. It had been a favorite back in Louisiana.

"Oh, buf-fa-lo gals, won't you come out to-night and dance by the light of the moon?"

Lian danced back to the two boys and eased between them. She took Andrew's right arm and Ned's left, then sang, "Buf-fa-lo gals, won't you come out to-night? Come out to-night? Come out to-night?"

Ned joined her. "Buf-fa-lo gals, won't you come out to-night—"

Then Andrew chimed in with, "—and dance by the light of the moon?"

"Ha!" Lian cried. She reached up and squeezed Andrew's cheek. "It's a fine morning! We're on a great adventure. What more could you want from life, eh, boys?"

Andrew and Ned agreed.

Lian looked down at the hand she had used to squeeze Andrew's cheek. "You're so sweaty!" Lian said, wiping her hand off on Andrew's shirt. "Yuck!"

"Thank you," Andrew said, shaking his head and causing sweat to fly at his companions. Lian pulled away from him and nearly tripped Ned. Then she stopped, threw back her head, and screamed at the top of her lungs. Andrew and Ned covered their ears.

"Why'd you do that?" Ned asked.

Lian shrugged. "Because I could. It's one of the reasons I love great open spaces. You can holler all you want, and no one thinks you're crazy!"

"Right," Andrew said. "We don't think you're crazy."

"Heck, no," Ned said.

"We *know* you're crazy!" the boys said in unison.

Lian laughed, then feinted back and aimed kicks at the air. "Laugh while you can, boys! *Hai!*"

Andrew looked over at Ned and smiled. The older boy returned the grin.

The trio soaked their faces with water from the canteens they carried, then put damp towels on their heads for protection against the sun.

Lian pointed toward a rise in the distance and asked, "Is that it?"

Andrew had seen Halcyon in his dreams the night before. In an excited whisper he said, "That's it."

After another half-hour of walking, the three friends reached the lost city and stood before the crumbling gates. The entrance was entirely blocked. Climbing the walls was the only way in.

Andrew squinted up at the walls, looking for the window. The sun was in the worst possible position. It sat above and behind the mountain housing the lost city, casting the area in shadow. Finally, Andrew pointed.

"I can't see a thing," Ned said.

Lian stepped forward. "I see it. Both of you stand clear." Lian muttered something in Chinese as she readied a device similar to a crossbow. It was loaded with a special bolt that had a grappling hook at its head. At the tail of the bolt was a hole not unlike the eye of a needle. A strong cord was knotted there. It was linked to a spool that Lian had set on the ground.

Lian took her time aiming for the spot of darkness—a patch of nightmare black against the dark gray of the ruins.

Ned suddenly spoke up. "Did I ever tell you how good I was at archery back in Louisiana?" he asked.

Lian shook her head.

"If you can't get it in three tries, I want a shot. Square?"

"Sure," said Lian. "If that's all right with Andrew."

The younger boy looked up in surprise. He'd been daydreaming about what they might find in the lost city. "Fine."

Lian smiled, her eyes still glued to the window. "But I'm not going to miss." She fired. The bolt sailed through the air, the cord unspooling behind it. She held her breath as the bolt passed directly through the window then slid back and clinked into place. She pulled on the cord, making sure it was taut.

"We're ready," she said.

"Wow, one shot," Ned said, shaking his head in amazement. "I couldn't have done that. 'Course, you've got more experience with these things than I do. Didn't you win a championship in climbing?"

Lian couldn't hide her smile. "Two, actually."

The rope was knotted at intervals of a foot and a half. Lian explained to the boys the best way to climb it.

"Watch me," she said. Putting on a pair of heavy

41

gloves, Lian started her ascent. "Use your hands and feet."

Lian effortlessly climbed the cord. In less than a minute she was at the ledge. She tested the stonework then climbed over, allowing one leg to dangle inside the lost city, the other outside.

"Can you see anything?" Andrew called up.

Lian peered into the darkness. "Nothing." She examined the ledge itself. "This is interesting! I just put my foot down and felt something. Some rocks must have fallen right about here. It might make getting down easier—I don't know. And there are marks in the stone ledge itself. Deep grooves. They could have been made by claws."

"That must be how the dinosaur climbed up," Andrew said.

"Andrew, you're next," Lian called.

Ned picked up one of the bags with their supplies and handed it to Andrew. The younger boy looped its strap over his head and shoulder. He began to shimmy up the cord.

Andrew was halfway up when Ned accidentally stepped on the free end of the cord, pulling it taut. Andrew screamed in surprise as the cord slipped from his fingers. Regaining his grip, Andrew hugged the cord and spun in place for a moment.

Ned hopped off the cord and looked up in dread. "Are you all right?" he cried.

"I'm okay," said Andrew, steeling his nerves. He

took a deep breath and shimmied the rest of the way up the cord. Lian helped him onto the ledge.

"All right," she said, pulling the cord up behind her. "I go down first. You wait here to pull the cord back up and throw it down to Ned."

Lian tossed the rope inside the lost city. She got a firm grip then quickly shimmied down. When Lian had reached the floor, Andrew hauled the rope back up. He repositioned the grappling hook and threw the line down to Ned.

"*Yeee-haaaa!*" Ned cried as he climbed the cord. The older boy kicked his legs out and made a show of climbing with only his hands. As he reached the ledge, Ned saw Andrew grinning. "I just always wanted to say that," explained Ned.

"You should be more careful," Andrew warned.

Ned chuckled. "I know. I'm sorry."

After Ned sat next to him on the ledge, Andrew repositioned the grappling hook and tossed the cord down to Lian. Taking a deep breath, he threw his legs over the side and started to climb down.

As Lian had advised, Andrew used both his hands and his feet. For a fleeting instant he thought about showing off the way Ned had, but he wasn't sure he could climb down with just his hands. As he descended, Andrew noticed that the air was surprisingly thin and clear, not musty as he'd expected.

"You're almost there," Lian coaxed.

Suddenly Andrew's feet struck solid ground. He'd

come down only about fifteen or twenty feet. He looked around but could see nothing.

"Your eyes will adjust," Lian said. "I think this was some kind of storeroom. It's filled with tables and chairs. And heavy boxes."

Andrew yanked on the cord. "Come on, Ned!"

Ned sat on the ledge, peering into the darkness. He'd done crazier things than this back in Louisiana. Back in the days before his father had decided to send him abroad for his education. In fact, he kind of missed those wild days.

With another joyous holler, Ned swung himself over the ledge without a thought to caution. Instantly, a sharp, terrible scraping sounded from over his head.

The hook! It was coming free!

Then the hook clanked firmly into place. Sighing heavily, Ned started to climb down the cord.

"Use your hands and feet!" Lian called.

"Right," said Ned. "I wasn't thinking."

Ned had climbed down two more feet when he heard the scraping sound again. He didn't even have time to scream as the grappling hook sprang loose and he found himself tumbling down into the darkness.

CHAPTER 8

Andrew heard Ned strike the floor. The older boy groaned.

"Ouch. That was pretty stupid," he said.

Andrew's eyes were adjusting to the darkness, just as Lian had said they would. He crouched down beside Ned. "Are you all right?" he asked.

Lian positioned herself on Ned's other side. "What's wrong?"

"It's my leg," Ned said, almost apologetically.

Lian examined Ned's leg. He gasped as she found the source of his pain.

"Your ankle's twisted," Lian said. "I don't think it's too bad, but it could be a sprain. We should find out for sure." Lian looked up at Andrew. "I'm sorry about your adventure, Andrew. We have to get Ned out of here."

"I know," Andrew said. The last thing he was thinking about right now was fun.

"Ned's supply bag must have slipped off when he fell," said Lian. "Do you see it anywhere?"

Andrew scanned the vast chamber. He could see shapes, but it was hard to make out the exact nature of each one. After rummaging about, he finally saw where the bag had fallen. Lian had already rounded up the cord and grappling hook. Andrew brought her the bag, and together they looked through it.

Lian found the crossbow device. It was snapped in two. She examined the grappling hook. Stones had fallen on it, flattening part of its clawlike grip. Both were useless.

"Looks like we're going to have to find another way out of here," Andrew said.

Ned was very quiet as Andrew and Lian searched the area, looking for something Ned could use as a walking stick. Finally, he said, "I'm really sorry about this."

"It's not your fault," Andrew replied.

Ned shook his head. "I shouldn't have been fooling around."

Suddenly a high, chittering sound burst from the darkness.

"What's that?" Andrew asked. The sounds rose up from every corner of the room.

Lian cocked her head to listen. "Andrew," she said, "whatever those things are, they're on every side of us. They seem small—"

"So they're no threat?" Andrew asked quickly.

"I'd like to think so," Lian said. "But I can name many predators that are also small."

"Okay," Andrew said. "Start upending those ta-bles. I'll do the same. We need to form a box around ourselves. Some kind of defense."

Andrew grabbed at the closest of the tables and turned it on its side. The corners of the room were immersed in total darkness. He could see nothing of the creatures making the noises. Lian dragged a table close.

"I can't stand not being able to help," Ned said.

"Just watch our backs," said Andrew.

"Right."

Lian and Andrew pulled several tables together, forming a small fort. The creatures were coming closer. Their chittering was growing louder.

Lian found three large sections of wood they could use as shields. With Andrew's help, Lian wrapped the straps from one of their supply bags around the wooden shield and secured it to her arm. Andrew did the same, though he knew the shield would offer no protection at all from the creature he had met on the road. Ned also fastened a shield to his arm.

Suddenly, one of the creatures sprang from the darkness. Lian saw snapping jaws. Tiny eyes. A body no larger than the length of her arm. She deflected it with her shield. Its weight made her rock back on her heels.

"Andrew—" she warned.

In an instant, they were under siege. The small

creatures leaped at their little fort, banging against the tables. Andrew deflected any of the creatures that made it over the top.

The tables moved again. Suddenly, one of the creatures flew right into Andrew's arms. The creature pawed up over Andrew's chest, its face over his—and started to lick him with a tiny, leathery tongue!

"What the—?" Andrew blurted out. The creature was patting Andrew's face with its tiny hands. Its tail beat a quick motion on his leg.

It was trying to play!

"Lian," Andrew said, holding the creature the way he might a puppy. "I'm going to name this one Happy. What do you think?"

Squinting, Lian turned and saw what had terrified them so much. She relaxed and allowed the tiny creatures to flood into their encampment. Andrew petted Happy's head. The creature's skull bobbed up and down, its lizardlike face content. Ned played with a couple of the creatures.

"You think it's possible we overreacted?" Lian asked.

"I think it's possible," Andrew replied.

"They're Compsognathus," Ned said. "Very young. Meat eaters, but so are a lot of our friends on Dinotopia. Technically, so are we."

Andrew rubbed Happy's belly. The creature cooed. "They sound like chickens. In fact, this seems to be a colony of chicks—"

Suddenly, a great roar sounded from the far end of the room. Happy leaped from Andrew's arms. The half-dozen or so Compsognathus that had entered the fort scattered. Their noises rose sharply then fell to an eerie silence.

Careful to keep herself hidden by the table, Lian peered around one corner and watched them go. She caught sight of a door at the far side of the room. There was a flickering golden-orange glow from the hall beyond. Someone had lit a torch and placed it in a brazier. The light silhouetted a figure in the doorway. Lian could see that it was not human. Sharp spikes protruded from its shoulders, and it stood on two spindly yet strong legs.

Lian blinked in confusion. Strangely, she was reminded of her father. The last time she had seen him, the man had been dressed as a warrior. He wore a helmet and a bizarre mask meant to frighten his enemies. Their family crest had been emblazoned on his clothing.

With a start Lian realized why this creature made her think of that final memory of her father: This creature was wearing *armor!*

CHAPTER 9

The armored figure came into the room and herded the Compsognathus out the way he'd come. The sounds from the Compsognathus and the creature leading them away quickly faded. The orange glow from the torch, however, remained in the hallway.

"Did you see it?" Andrew whispered.

Lian looked over. Andrew had been peering around the other side of the tables. Ned was grumbling to himself. He tried to get to his feet on his own but couldn't make it.

"I saw it," she said.

"We have to be careful," Andrew warned.

Lian nodded as all three removed their shields. "If we stay here, the window is our only chance for escape," she said.

"We could try stacking the tables high enough to reach the window," Andrew suggested. "But it looks as if most of them are falling apart."

"And we'd still have to worry about climbing down to the ground," Lian said. "If we tied one end of the cord to something, we could lower ourselves down."

"I don't know. I don't see anything in this room I'd trust with my life," said Andrew.

"What we need is to find some other equipment," added Ned.

"I agree," Lian said. "We'll have to explore the city. Of course, there are the chicken herders to consider. You think the one we just saw was the same one you met on the road?"

"I don't know," said Andrew. "I think we should try to watch them, see what they're like. If worst comes to worst, we can always ask them for help."

Andrew and Lian searched the room again and found a large stick that Ned could use as a crutch. The two got on either side of Ned and helped him up. He leaned on Lian and the stick, doing his best not to put full pressure on his injured ankle.

They reached the doorway, Andrew taking the lead. He peered around the corner. A lit torch sat in a brazier near the doorway. At the far end of the corridor, another flickered in the shadows.

"The dinosaur must have lit the torches as he came this way," Andrew said. "That gives us a trail to follow."

"A trail leading right back to our friend with the armor," Ned said.

Lian nodded. "He's right. We should take one of the torches and explore the areas that are unlit."

"Good idea," Andrew said. He picked up the nearer torch and led the way. The corridor was lined with hieroglyphics. Many of the drawings showed dinosaurs like the one they'd just seen. In the drawings they were huddled together or playing games, and odd symbols were scrawled around the images. Lian pointed at them.

"Do you think this is a written language?" she asked.

"Probably," Andrew said. "This is incredible. I wonder what stories these people have to tell?"

"I don't know," said Ned. "I just hope we can find a way out."

Fragments of pots and dishes, along with broken wooden tools, lined the edges of the walkway. None of the trio could figure out what the tools had been used for.

"I get the feeling the residents avoid this section of the city," Andrew said.

Lian agreed. They came to a fork in the corridor and followed the unlit path.

Soon they passed into another section of the ruins. The corridors were wider. Ornately carved stone columns came into view. A fantastic mural was painted on a nearby wall. The three went over to look at it.

"It's an octopus, or squid, or something," Lian said, referring to the huge creature at the center of the mural. "And it seems to have its tentacles around men and dinosaurs."

"It looks like something from one of Andrew's stories," said Ned.

"You're right," Andrew said, looking at the image thoughtfully.

With a last look at the mural, they started off again. Soon they came to a narrow corridor. At the end of the corridor were several steps up to a landing. The way back down on the opposite side was blocked by fallen stone. They went into a tiny room off to the side, then made a series of sharp rights, lefts, several more rights—

"We're in a maze," Ned said.

Andrew shook his head. "I don't think so. These rooms and halls were designed for a purpose. We just don't know what it is."

The trio stumbled around until they finally found their way out of the labyrinth. They walked down a little flight of stairs that had been partially blocked and came out into a large courtyard. To one side were beautifully designed thrones that had been chipped from the stone walls. Ned sat down to rest on one of them for a few moments.

"I keep thinking about that painting," Andrew said. "It reminds me of cautionary tales that I've heard. You know, like the one about the fire imps that warn little kids not to play too close to fire. The picture looked like a warning of some sort. 'This is something we're afraid of. You should be afraid too.' Yet we're too far from the coast for sea creatures of that size. I don't get it, do you?"

Neither Lian nor Ned had any idea.

The remains of beautifully decorated jugs and basins littered the floor. At her feet, Lian saw an ancient bronze hair curler and beside it a chipped steel helmet. Andrew discovered bronze utensils, spiral arm rings, and several large broken stools meant to allow certain dinosaurs the luxury of sitting.

Andrew scanned the courtyard. "With so much stuff scattered around, we're bound to find what we need to get out of here."

They found two pottery kilns, more broken jugs, and bits of weaponry, but nothing that would help them. Lian stopped before a bronze tripod carrying a cracked basin.

"That's a spindle whorl," Lian said, pointing to a large machine across the room. "You use it to spin thread. I wonder what it's doing here?"

"I think this entire area is a dumping ground," Andrew said. "A waste heap. We haven't even gotten close to Halcyon's residents."

Ned scooped up something near him. "Look at this. Coins with human and Saurian faces."

"This *is* an ancient place, isn't it?" Lian said. "Dinotopians barter; they don't use money anymore."

Soon they passed through five winding, interlocking corridors. Occasionally they found a door, but never one that was open.

"I wonder where we are?" Andrew said. "What do you think this part of Halcyon used to be?"

"I don't know," said Lian. "Henna told me that

this city existed before the Dinotopians turned away from the ways of the warrior."

"It must be true," said Ned. "Look at all the pieces of weapons and armor lying around."

Andrew nodded. "So this area was probably the guards' quarters. It makes sense."

"A good guess," Lian said. "As good as any."

Ned cleared his throat. "Do either of you hear that weird noise?"

Andrew nodded. He had been hearing odd sounds for some time now. They were muted through the heavy stone walls. Thunderous roars echoing from somewhere near. The clang of steel upon steel.

They came to another door. This time they tried it. The door was locked. Sighing, Andrew dug into his pocket and nervously fingered the armlet he'd found.

"What's wrong?" Lian asked.

Andrew shrugged. "I wish I hadn't stayed so late in the city. If I had just picked up the goods for Father and the celebration, maybe none of this would have happened. We'd all be safe right now, and Ned wouldn't be hurt."

"I'm not hurt that bad," said Ned. "Besides, this is exciting. And if anyone's to blame for us being trapped here, it's me with my *yee-hawwws*. But the point is, blaming ourselves isn't going to do any good. We've got to 'keep our eyes on the prize,' as my daddy used to say."

"I couldn't agree more," Lian said.

Andrew nodded, feeling better. "Agreed."

Ned said that his ankle felt better, and he wanted to try to get along with just the walking stick. He was slow at first, but both Lian and Andrew were relieved to see him getting around more easily. Then the group turned another corner and froze.

Two heavily armored dinosaurs stood directly before them. The dinosaurs did not appear to see the three humans. They each held long staffs with curved blades. Both appeared to be frozen in place.

Andrew stared at the dinosaurs. They had long tails and bright orange eyes with catlike slits. Their long snouts held more teeth than any other dinosaur, and their claws had odd little hooks.

They were Troodons, like Malik and the dinosaur Andrew had seen on the road!

Andrew took in the armor that each dinosaur wore. Ridged helmets were fitted over their long, reptilian skulls. Chain mail protected their necks. Their chestplates, or cuirasses, were Asian in design, with dragonlike faces covering their shoulders and upper arms. Brightly colored sashes were wrapped around their waists. Steel spikes protruded from their hips. Plates were fitted over their knees.

A copper dagger hung from the waist sash of one dinosaur; a long ax with a nasty-looking blade was held in reserve by the other. Andrew looked at the dinosaur's lower arms. The dinosaur wearing a red sash had an armlet for each appendage. His opponent, whose sash was green, had only one—and it was a perfect match for the one in Andrew's hand!

The two faced each other down. One of them finally moved. The other gave a mighty roar. In an instant, the blades on their long staffs crashed together.

Their movements were sharp and quick. The dinosaurs had to put their entire bodies into swinging and dropping their blades. Red Sash attacked with a right-to-left diagonal cut. Green Sash dropped back, shifting his weight onto his right leg, easing his weapon down onto his thigh. Then he advanced with his right leg and arm, his leg supporting the weight as he smashed the weapon of his opponent toward the dinosaur's face. Red Sash fell back, pirouetted, and spun the weapon for another attack, which was easily countered.

Andrew whispered, "We'd better go back the way we came. Maybe later, when it's dark—"

"No," said Lian.

Ned looked at her in surprise. "What?"

Lian took a step forward and said, "The two of you should go back. I have to try and talk to them. This is what I was hoping to find. I can't turn my back on it now."

"It might not be safe," Andrew said.

"I'm willing to risk it," Lian responded firmly.

Andrew looked to Ned. "What about you?"

"I think we should stay with her."

Andrew nodded. "All right. But now doesn't look

57

like the best time. Maybe we should talk to them later, when they're *not fighting!*"

A sudden, complete silence rose up around them. The three young humans turned to see the Troodons staring at them!

For a moment, no one moved. Then Andrew remembered the armlet he'd found. With a trembling hand, he held it out. The dinosaur who had been missing an armlet stalked forward. Reaching out with sharp claws, he took the beautiful metal and slipped it on, nodding.

Both dinosaurs took a step back and gestured for the humans to follow them. They set their staffs against the wall and put their hands at their sides.

"What do you think?" asked Andrew. "Do we go with them, or try to run?"

"I know I'm not up to playing hide-and-seek," said Ned.

"This is what we came here for," said Lian. "An adventure."

"All right," said Andrew.

As the group moved forward, one of the dinosaurs fell in behind them while the other led the way.

"Say, Andrew," Ned whispered. "You said you wanted to come here to get a story, right?"

"Right."

"Well," said Ned as they followed the warrior Troodon, "I think we're about to get a real good one."

CHAPTER 10

Until this moment, Andrew, Lian, and Ned had been in the dark ruins on the edge of Halcyon. Now they were walking into the light.

The mountain into which Halcyon had been dug was chosen for a reason. It was extremely treacherous, making it the ideal location for a fortress. Large holes had been made in the top of the mountain, allowing the people of Halcyon a view of the sky.

As the three were led through the city, they saw several other Troodons engaged in matches like the one they had interrupted. Here, near the city's center, the buildings were well maintained. The architecture was a blend of many styles, with Roman round archways leading to vast chambers with Gothic rib-vaulted ceilings.

Statues of dinosaurs were everywhere. They passed a garden where the hedges had been cut into the shapes of warrior dinosaurs and a few of the other species. Shining fountains had white glistening dinosaur statues spouting water.

Totem poles with the features of Troodons reduced to blocky representations were everywhere. Atop each was a huge lizard perched on four paws, looking down inquisitively. Andrew was fascinated. This was like walking through a fairy tale world.

They were taken through a set of double doors and saw that a large bowl-shaped arena stretched out before them. Warriors competed below while hundreds of Troodons watched. In the stands, a number of Troodons had painted their bodies with white and black stripes. Their helms sprouted long horns topped off with fluffy pink feathers. These dinosaurs made odd, jerky motions as they circulated through the crowds.

They were clowns! Andrew realized.

Other dinosaurs raced through the field below. They were short and squat, unlike the Troodons—or so Andrew thought at first. Then he realized that they were simply Troodons wearing bulky costumes of other dinosaurs from the island. The onlookers laughed at them, especially when they came too close to the dueling warriors and were jokingly driven off. The roaring laughter was strange but beautiful.

Andrew, Lian, and Ned were led around the outer rim of the arena. The Troodons in the audience did not seem to notice them. Andrew saw a Troodon female, or so he guessed from her soft robes and flowery headdress. She had a large cap of scented wax on her head, which gave off an intoxicating perfume as the heat made it melt. Other Troodons wore gigantic, plumed headdresses of all styles and colors. They wore turquoise necklaces with spiral patterns, beads, and shiny metal chestplates formed from squares that reached out from a single point and grew ever larger.

It was all so strange. But so fantastic!

"Is this how you solve disagreements?" Andrew asked. "Trial by combat? Or is there some other reason for these games?"

The Troodon leading him said something in response, but Andrew couldn't understand him.

Before Andrew could see any more, he and the others were led through a door at the back of the coliseum and down a shadowy corridor. The roars of the crowd and the crashing of steel upon steel quickly faded. They came to a torchlit room with a huge statue at the rear.

The Troodons left them.

"This is really amazing," Andrew said. "Lian, what do you think they were doing in the arena?"

"Testing themselves," she said distantly. "There was no anger. That's what was so strange. They're fierce, but not angry. It all seemed like steps to a dance. Like a ceremony."

"I wonder why they hide themselves away here," said Ned.

"They might not be hiding at all," said Andrew. "They might not realize what's outside these walls."

The doors suddenly burst open. A pageant of

brightly dressed Troodons entered the room. Some took positions near the door. Others carried torches.

"Now we should get some answers," Andrew said.

"Let's hope," Ned replied.

Three Troodons wore golden armor trimmed in crimson. They seemed to be the ones in charge.

The doors opened one last time, admitting a small, gray Bagaceratops that idled toward the humans. The dinosaur had a horned face. His hide was so thick and granite-like that he looked like a statue of a pig waddling to life. His tail was as heavy and thick as a club. He said, "I am Grizzardle. I speak both the common Dinotopian languages and the more evolved and refined language of the Unrivaled—"

"The Unrivaled?" Andrew asked.

"The Troodons. It is their name for themselves." The small dinosaur cleared his throat. "It is my duty to welcome newcomers. Not that there have ever been newcomers—not so long as I can recall. The last one, I think, was me! And that was forty years ago! Forgive me, I'm very excited. I'm practically at a loss for words. I was beginning to think my talents would never come in handy."

Andrew started to relax. "So no one's upset that we're here?"

"Good gracious, no!" cried the Bagaceratops. "This is your time, that's all. And there's a time for everything, and everything in its time. That's one of the many codes the Unrivaled live by. You'll get used to their way of doing things soon enough. And I'm sure they'll get used to yours, too. They're quite a fine tribe, I must say."

"So it's okay if we wanted to, um, leave, right?" asked Andrew.

"Of course!" said Grizzardle. "Though I can't imagine why you'd want to. Who would, once one had experienced the most civilized, most highly evolved society on Dinotopia?"

Andrew tried to hide his grin. He looked over at Lian with raised eyebrows.

She smiled back. "I *would* like some time with these Saurians," she said.

The younger boy looked at Ned.

"It's all right with me," Ned said.

Andrew turned back to Grizzardle and bowed. "Okay. You've got some houseguests for a while."

"Delightful!" said the Bagaceratops. "Simply delightful!" He turned to the Troodons and said something to them in their language.

All the Troodons in the chamber began talking at once, nodding their heads and banging their shields in approval. In the midst of all this noise and activity, Ned stepped forward and slapped Andrew on the back. "Great job, Andrew!" he said.

The sound of the blow seemed to echo in the suddenly silent chamber. The Troodons stared at Ned and Andrew in horror. The humans watched as their horror turned slowly to anger. Throughout the chamber, the Troodons began muttering to each other. In their eyes, Andrew saw the fierceness he'd first seen in the eyes of the hooded Troodon that rainy night.

"Um—excuse me?" Andrew said. "What's going on?"

Grizzardle seemed panicked.

"What?" Ned cried. "What did I do?"

"This is bad, very bad," said Grizzardle as he listened to the frantic exchanges of the Troodons.

"Please," said Andrew. "Tell us what's wrong!"

Grizzardle shook his head and lowered his gaze. "Your friend just committed a criminal offense."

Ned's jaw dropped. "Now, wait a minute! That doesn't make any sense. We've seen you run around with swords, fighting each other with deadly weapons—"

"Appearances can be deceiving," Grizzardle warned.

"—and I'm in trouble because I gave Andrew a friendly slap on the back?"

"They don't see such contact as friendly," said the Bagaceratops. "And, no, you're not in trouble."

"Well, good!" Ned said.

"Actually, it's *all three* of you who are in trouble...."

CHAPTER 11

The Troodon council fell into a heated debate over what to do about the humans. Grizzardle kept Andrew, Ned, and Lian informed as best he could while answering their questions.

"The Rituals of the Art—what you unenlightened might call the rules of personal combat—serve a high purpose," Grizzardle explained. "The greatest crime in the Unrivaled's society is to strike someone. It is simply unthinkable."

"Now, come on," Ned interrupted. "Those two who were fighting with the staffs and the hooked blades? And all of the warriors in the arena with their swords and shields? That was all friendly?"

"As a matter of fact," said the Bagaceratops, "it was. Only a Master of the Art is allowed a weapon with a cutting edge. Both are participants in a Flourish—"

"A what?" asked Lian.

"A Flourish," said the gray dinosaur. "I believe you uncivilized types call it a duel. Now, I'm willing to impart this rare and exalted knowledge on the condition that I am not *interrupted* every few sentences!"

Ned and the others fell silent.

"Thank you," Grizzardle said. "The whole point of becoming a master is to gain supreme control, enough to never land a blow anywhere except against the sword or shield of your partner."

"Then how does anyone win?" asked Lian.

Grizzardle sighed. "The moment it becomes clear that a warrior's defenses can be breached, the match is ended by mutual consent."

Lian shook her head, thinking of her homeland and her family's warrior ways. "But what if the Unrivaled had to go up against a real enemy? What if they had to defend the lives of others? Would they do what's necessary?"

"Harming another is never what's necessary," said Grizzardle. "It can always be avoided. For those who don't believe that, those who willingly strike another—"

Ned frowned at this.

"—there is severe punishment."

The Bagaceratops gestured for the trio to wait as he listened to the Unrivaled's debate. He butted in on their conversation, adding something in an imploring tone. They responded, and he sighed and turned away.

"What are they saying?" asked Andrew.

"They are weighing their options," said the gray dinosaur.

Andrew tried to control the anger and fear building up inside him. "Doesn't it matter that I'm not hurt, that I'm not upset with Ned? It was a friendly gesture between us."

"I know," said Grizzardle. "I lived among the Realms Without for many years before retiring to Halcyon."

Ned came forward. "And now that I know that it's against your laws, I promise I'll never do it again."

"Ah," said the gray dinosaur wearily. "Unfortunately, ignorance of the law cannot be an excuse."

"Fine," said Ned. "Then we'll just leave."

"That is always your choice." Grizzardle said.

"No," said Lian firmly. "I don't want to leave. I want to learn from the...Unrivaled, as you call them. Here I may be able to train as a warrior. In my homeland, I wanted to be a warrior but couldn't."

Grizzardle cocked his head. "Why not?"

"Because I'm a female," Lian said.

"And?"

"That's it."

The gray dinosaur sighed. "The Realms Without seem to operate without rhyme or reason."

"You don't mean the rest of Dinotopia, too, do you?" asked Andrew.

"We are content here," was all Grizzardle said in answer. "We have all we need. Food. Warmth. Companionship. Music. And our devotion to the Art."

Lian struggled to understand. "But what good is

being a warrior if you don't have an enemy to fight?"

"Ignorance is as good an enemy as any," said Grizzardle. "Intolerance. Injustice."

"But how do you fight these things?" asked Lian. "No one even knows your culture exists! Why do you hide away?"

"Who's hiding?" asked Grizzardle. "There's a difference between hiding and choosing not to venture forth."

"What about this punishment you were talking about?" Andrew asked. "There's nothing forcing us to go along with your decision."

"Actually, as long as you stay here, there's no avoiding it," said Grizzardle. "The only punishment severe enough for the crime of violence is the Great Silence."

"What's that?" asked Andrew.

"If someone breaks our most revered law, that no being shall strike or harm another, he is shunned for a period of one year. No one prevents him from taking food or finding a comfortable place to live. But, by the same token, no one is allowed to communicate with him or in any way acknowledge his existence."

"Oh," said Andrew, realizing that this was indeed a sentence they could do nothing about.

"This punishment has been enforced only a few times in the Unrivaled's history. There have never been repeat offenders."

"Why don't the Troodons who've done something wrong just leave?" asked Andrew.

"Leave?" said Grizzardle. "Unthinkable. No punishment is severe enough to make someone want to leave. Ours is the most evolved society this island has ever seen. The thought of a citizen voluntarily leaving is simply ridiculous!"

Andrew couldn't help but think of the Troodon he'd met on the road—the one whose armband he'd found and returned. Why had he left the city if it was so perfect?

Suddenly, the golden-robed Troodons stood before Andrew and his friends. They began to speak. Andrew was surprised to find that he could actually understand a word or two. Was it possible that the Troodons' language was similar to his own?

Grizzardle translated. "Our uninvited guests are complete innocents, with no knowledge whatsoever of the ways of the truly civilized society. We understand this and forgive their trespass this one time. Our judgment, the Great Silence, will be waived—provided they are willing to leave their innocence behind and become civilized."

"Civilized?" Andrew asked.

"Stay with us," Grizzardle explained. "Learn from us. Let us teach you what is important in life. See what it is like to engage in our competitions."

"We've been in lots of competitions," said Ned. He went on to describe the events he had been in in the Dinosaur Olympics. Grizzardle was intrigued. He went back to the Troodons, who spoke among themselves for a few moments. Then the little gray dinosaur came forward.

"We thank you!" said Grizzardle. "We were wondering how to decide to which houses we would assign you."

"What are you talking about?" asked Andrew. "You want to split us up?"

"Oh, yes!" said Grizzardle. "Each of you will be taken to a different house, of course. There you will be taught proper conduct. You will learn what is important in life."

"Why separately?" asked Andrew.

"If you stay together at this critical time, you will cling to each other and to your old beliefs."

Ned swallowed hard. He hoped that he hadn't just gotten them into worse trouble. "You said we solved this problem for you?"

"Yes," said Grizzardle. "We will put you in a contest with some of our warriors. Don't worry, you won't be hurt. We'll be very gentle."

"So what will these contests determine?" asked Lian.

"We will gauge your abilities," Grizzadle said. "Then we will be able to tell to which house you will each be most suited!"

"But we don't have to go along with this?" Andrew said.

"No, of course not," said Grizzardle. "We would never think of inflicting our will on others. But you must make a choice. If you refuse our generous terms, this will be the last time any citizen of Halcyon will speak to you or acknowledge your existence. Ever."

Andrew turned to his friends. "We'd better talk about this."

The three quickly agreed that even if they found what they needed to reach the window and climb out, they might not be able to find their way back to the window. The city was such a maze. And even if they could find another way out, it would still be a shame not to learn as much as possible about the Unrivaled.

Andrew looked to his friends one last time. Ned and Lian nodded.

"All right," Andrew said. "Teach us."

CHAPTER 12

Before long, two Troodon escorts led Andrew, Ned, and Lian to the testing grounds.

"I am reminded of the Way of the Warrior," Lian said to her friends. "In China, and Japan especially, it is called the Bushido. It is the strict code by which a samurai serves his master. But these warriors seem to serve no one but themselves. They are Ronin. Masterless warriors. Yet they seem content. It is strange."

The three humans were taken to a wide chamber that held two identical obstacle courses. The rules, as Grizzardle explained, were simple. The first combatant to pass through the gates at the end of the room would win.

"You have a choice," said the Bagaceratops. "You can run this course or the maze below. Choose now."

Ned rolled up his sleeves. The course consisted of logs raised about four feet off the ground, spaced at irregular intervals, with poles and many other obstructions placed in the runner's way.

"I'll run this course," Ned said. Andrew nodded

and said he would too. Lian chose the maze.

"Very well. Good luck!" said the little gray dinosaur. Then he went off with Lian and a handful of Troodons.

Andrew turned to Ned. "How's the leg?" he asked. "Are you sure you're ready for this?"

"I feel just fine," said Ned. "Doesn't hurt at all. I think all the walking helped."

Andrew and Ned took a moment to look over the closest of the two identical obstacle courses.

"Have you noticed the way the Troodons move?" asked Ned. "Their backs don't bend. It's as if they have steel rods in them. So that means they can't crouch; they can't move their shoulders one way, their hips another. We may be able to take advantage of that. Maybe in that area about halfway through."

Andrew saw what Ned meant. That section of the course contained several odd skeletal constructs that looked like buildings with only support beams, no walls or ceilings.

"These guys are pretty sure of themselves," said Ned. "But I'm gonna show 'em how it's done."

Ned's opponent turned out to be the warrior Andrew had met on the road, the owner of the armlet Andrew had found.

The Troodon stepped forward to introduce himself.

"Arri," the Troodon said, patting his own chest. It came out "Arrghh-reeee."

There was a neutral area between the two courses, so that there would be no contact between those being tested. Andrew watched as Arri took his place at the beginning of his course and Ned did the same on the other course.

Arri pointed to another Troodon carrying a horn. He motioned that when the horn was sounded, they were expected to run.

Ned nodded tensely.

A few seconds later, the signal was given. Ned ran toward the logs. He glanced over to the other course and was startled to see Arri already ahead of him. The Troodon leaped up onto the four-foot-high logs with perfect grace. He jumped from one to another very quickly, running into problems only when he had to turn at a sharp angle.

Ned was determined not to fail. Instead of trying to climb the logs, he either leaped over them or slid beneath them. Soon he had recovered the lead. When they reached the wide-open log cabins, Arri climbed the logs. Ned went through them.

Realizing that the human's flexibility was providing serious competition, Arri made it to the top of the log cabin and down again in two quick leaps. When Arri landed, he was a good deal ahead of his human opponent.

After that, there was really no contest.

Although Ned was a natural athlete, the course was wearing him down. The Troodon didn't have this problem. Arri's stamina was astounding. He reached the end of the course thirty seconds before Ned did.

Breathing heavily, Ned leaned back on one of the logs and folded his arms over his chest. He was startled that he could have lost. He never lost at things like this. What was happening here?

"Come on, Ned!" called Andrew. "Finish the race."

"It is finished," said Ned. With a disappointed sigh, he walked the rest of the course and passed through the gate. Arri held out his claw to Ned. The older boy did not take it. He could not believe he had *lost!*

Soon, it was Andrew's turn. He stood at the beginning of the course and looked over to find that Arri would also be his opponent!

This is crazy, Andrew thought. The Troodons built this course. They're faster and stronger. Look at the way they can jump—twice their height if they need to! Who knows how many times Arri's run this course? If *Ned* couldn't beat him, how can *I* compete?

One of the judges signaled for the competition to begin. Andrew gritted his teeth and ran straight ahead, then suddenly saw a way that he might win after all....

Meanwhile, Lian was led down several winding passages to a dark set of tunnels far below the city. She could hear the sound of rushing waters somewhere nearby. Grizzardle explained that a waterway ran beneath the city, supplying power as well as fish.

Lian's task was to enter the maze before her and find her way through to the other side. Na'dra, her opponent, would enter the maze from another point and attempt to beat her to the finish.

At certain points the two mazes intersected. Lian might turn a corner and find Na'dra waiting for her. Or she could choose to wait and ambush the Troodon, taking the chance that the warrior had already passed that way and was completing the maze.

"What happens if we do meet up?" Lian asked.

"You or she may throw one of these," said Grizzardle. He nodded in the direction of a Troodon warrior. The dinosaur stepped forward and handed Lian three large red cloth rings.

Grizzardle continued. "If she manages to throw one of these over your head—"

"Like a lasso!" said Lian.

"What?"

"Something Ned described to me once."

"Ah. Well, if it passes over your head or around your arm and stays there, you must stop and count to one hundred before continuing. The same goes for her if you toss the ring."

"What's to prevent me from removing the cloth and saying she missed?" asked Lian.

"I don't understand."

"I'm saying someone could cheat."

Grizzardle tried to understand this. Finally, he gave up and said, "You humans are very peculiar."

Lian grinned. Apparently, cheating was something so unfamiliar to the Unrivaled that they didn't even understand it. She was beginning to really like them.

One of the Troodons handed her a torch. She said, "I don't know if I want this."

Grizzardle said, "You'll be blind in the tunnels without the torch."

"Will Na'dra have a torch?" Lian asked.

"She won't need one. Her vision will adjust."

'Then she'll be able to see me from a distance, but I won't be able to see her!"

'Perhaps. Perhaps not. The torch will put you on a more equal footing with her. Now take off your shoes."

Lian hesitated.

"It is part of the rules," Grizzardle said. "If you don't comply, you will forfeit. Then how will we know which house best suits you?"

Shaking her head, Lian removed her shoes. She took her place, waited until the signal was given, then started forward through the maze.

In a room far above Lian, Andrew had just started the obstacle course. He made it over the first few logs easily enough, but paused at a five-foot-high wooden dinosaur. He was supposed to vault over this obstacle, and he wanted Arri to believe that he couldn't do it.

The Troodon was running through the course very easily. Arri had not only jumped over several flat wooden dinosaurs, he was on a second set of logs, making a show of leaping from log to log. Confident that his opponent was no match for him, the Troodon was caught up in the beauty of his own performance.

Andrew couldn't have been more pleased. He made his move.

Arri had just landed another amazing leap when one of the judges cried out. Arri looked over to see the human boy passing the last obstacle and racing toward the finish line!

Stunned, Arri realized what had happened. The human had taken the rules of the contest at their precise word: Whoever passes the finish line first, wins. There was nothing in the rules that actually stated that one had to go through the obstacles to get there. Andrew was ignoring the obstacles and running along the neutral area dividing the courses!

Brilliant, Arri thought, as he jumped to the ground and raced after the human. As brilliant as his own overconfident display had been foolish.

Lian peered ahead cautiously. A part of her dearly wanted to prove herself to the Unrivaled. A warrior society here on Dinotopia! How unlikely—and how wonderful! It appeared that her dream of becoming a true warrior might actually come to pass.

She moved forward. The tunnel branched to the right and the left.

Think, she told herself. This is a test of skill, not luck. There is a way to know which path to take.

She studied the walls. There were no markings to show her the way. The ceiling was also barren. Damp gray stone walls surrounded her.

Suddenly Lian realized that the floor was not smooth. Why had they asked her to run this maze in her bare feet?

Lian looked down and smiled.

She knew the answer.

Lian felt along the floor with the soles of her feet. The floor was cut into a series of ridges that led along the tunnel she was on, then veered off to the left-hand passage.

Lian decided that this "path" had been placed here to confuse her and slow her down. She was willing to gamble that she wasn't in a maze at all. No matter what route she took, she would end up at the finish line.

Lian took the right-hand tunnel, racing forward until the corridor split three ways. She continued along the most center route, connected to five more tunnels, and again chose the tunnel in the middle. Lian wagered that she was traveling the most direct route to the finish line. The thunderous roars of the water crashing against the walls was deafening.

As she ran, Lian thought of her torch. She wondered how she could turn it to her advantage. Grizzardle had said that Na'dra's eyes would adjust to the darkness. Maybe the light from the torch would be bright enough to temporarily blind Na'dra. Then Lian could throw one of the circles around her opponent's neck!

Lian plunged forward, turned a corner, and saw a sharp movement. Surprised, she shoved the torch out before her. A loud cry sounded above the crashing of the waters. A tail slapped against the wall. Limbs flailed. Scales and armor and orange glowing eyes flashed.

Na'dra was here!

The Troodon grabbed at her face and turned from Lian. The young human was horrified. Had she accidently burned the Troodon? She knew that if she wanted to win, she had to throw the red cloth ring now, while Na'dra was disoriented. But what if the dinosaur was hurt?

Lowering the torch, Lian said, "Are you all right? Let's forget the competition. I'll help you get to the front, and we'll go through the line together—"

Na'dra turned suddenly. With a cry of laughter and triumph, the Troodon whipped out her free claw and tossed one of the cloth circles. It fell neatly around Lian's head.

Lian clenched her fists in frustration. She'd been fooled by one of the oldest tricks in the book. Angry with herself, Lian started to count.

Na'dra took Lian's torch, cried out a strange phrase, then raced down the corridor. Her light quickly vanished.

*   *   *

Meanwhile, Andrew was in sight of the finish line. He could hear Arri behind him, quickly closing the gap.

With a last burst of speed, Andrew raced past the finish seconds before Arri. Nearly a dozen Troodons looked on in stunned silence. Gasping for breath, Andrew felt someone touch his shoulder. Turning, he saw it was Arri. The Troodon reached out and gave Andrew's arm a firm squeeze, then he drew back, bowed, and began to clap.

One of the Troodons sounded a horn twice. Another handed Andrew a sash. Then the rest of the Troodons in the chamber began clapping.

"I can't believe it," Andrew said as Ned came over. "I won! I've never won anything!"

Ned nodded slowly. "Looks like your luck's changing," he said.

Then Arri threw back his head and sang a song of praise to the victor. His fellow warriors joined in.

In the tunnels below, Lian emerged at her own finish line to find Grizzardle and two escorts waiting.

The victor had long since collected her prize and been ushered away.

Grizzardle cocked his head at Lian. "So, you lost," he said.

Lian shrugged.

"And how does this make you feel?"

"I'm not thrilled, but it was a fair contest," she

said. Then Lian repeated the phrase Na'dra had said to her and asked its meaning.

"Strategy is everything," said the dinosaur.

Lian laughed. "I'll remember that next time."

"Come, Lian," said Grizzardle. "I think I know where you'll be happy."

CHAPTER 13

The following days were filled with both difficulties and wonders.

Directly after the competition, Andrew said goodbye to his friends for the time being. He felt energized by his victory. If this could happen, anything was possible!

Within an hour he found himself at the home of Lord Botolf, the Troodon knight who would supervise his training. Andrew's achievement and his shrewd use of strategy had brought him to Botolf's notice.

Andrew saw little of the house as he was ushered in a side entrance and down a flight of winding stairs. At the bottom was a dark chamber with very few furnishings.

Grizzardle was already there, along with Arri. The Troodon came forward and embraced Andrew. Then he stepped back and bowed. Andrew bowed in return.

A torch burned in a brazier on the wall behind Andrew, giving off a flickering amber light. Andrew stood before the Troodon, fascinated by the way the fire seemed to dance in the warrior's eyes.

Arri was bold, like Ned, Andrew thought. Andrew admired that quality and wondered if his victory meant he possessed a little of it himself!

Grizzardle cleared his throat to get Andrew's attention. "To begin with," he said, "this house is where you will stay while you are with us. The Unrivaled would greatly appreciate it if you do not venture out on your own yet. Arri will take you wherever you need to go."

"Okay," said Andrew.

"However, they would also prefer that you spend the remainder of this day within this room. Your meals and whatever else you need will be brought to you. Um—you do like fish, don't you?"

"Sounds wonderful."

"Good," said Grizzardle. "There is much for you to learn. Arri will be your companion, if that's all right with you—"

"Sure!" Andrew said, grinning at the Troodon.

"The two of you must learn to communicate when no one else is around. It is the same with Lian and Ned and their companions. There is only one of me and three of you."

Andrew nodded.

"Now, I considered this problem long ago," said Grizzardle. "I came up with six basic commands that you must learn. Arri? If you would?"

Nodding, Arri went to a table at the far end of the room and retrieved six scrolls. Hand gestures were drawn on the scrolls, their meanings written beneath them.

"You see," said the little gray dinosaur, "I've had plenty of time to devise a program for my students. In truth, these scrolls have been collecting dust for years. Study them well."

Andrew looked at the scrolls. The gestures were very basic: One finger to the mouth stood for SILENCE. Bringing two fingers near the eye and then sharply pulling them away meant AVERT GAZE. A slight flourish with one claw meant BOW, DON'T SMILE. Two fingers set at the side of the head and aimed straight ahead meant STARE BOLDLY. Two fingers, one walking before the other meant TIME TO LEAVE. Two fingers moving back and forth quickly meant TOUCH NOTHING.

"I'm off to see your friends," said Grizzardle. "I'll return later to quiz you."

"Wait a minute," Andrew said. "You don't have to come back later. I understand the signals now."

"Really?" asked Grizzardle. "The Compsognathus still don't get it!"

Andrew quickly went through the gestures and their meanings without looking at the study guides.

"Hmmph!" said the Bagaceratops approvingly. "Clever. But will you still remember them in an hour?"

"You've been away from humans for a very long time, haven't you?" Andrew asked.

"Forty years," said the dinosaur.

Andrew smiled. "Why don't we also try to come up with gestures for when I need to ask or do something?"

Grizzardle nodded. "I suppose I could have more paper brought."

"And another thing," Andrew continued. "It seems as if the Troodons' language might just be an older form of what we're speaking."

"You noticed that."

Andrew nodded.

"Are your friends as bright as you are?"

"I'd say so," Andrew said. "Grizzardle, I have so many questions about the Unrivaled—"

"I'm sure you do," said Grizzardle. "Everything will be made clear to you in time."

Andrew nodded. There was no need to press any harder.

That day, Andrew and Arri worked hard to understand each other and devise their own form of silent communication. Grizzardle returned after nightfall and was surprised at how well Andrew was learning the Unrivaled's language. Andrew explained that as long as the Troodons spoke slowly and clearly, he could understand many familiar words.

Lord Botolf, Andrew's host, was informed of Andrew's progress. Word was sent that Botolf wished to wait until Andrew was more comfortable with the Troodon language before arranging a meeting. On the whole, the Troodon knight was very pleased with his new arrival's progress.

The next day, Andrew was allowed to go into the city with Arri. As they walked, Arri explained to him why the Troodons did not want Andrew and his friends to explore the city unsupervised. The Troodons, the most agile and intelligent of the Saurians, looked on humans as Andrew might a small child. He could picture a curious child touching something he wasn't supposed to, like a weapon, and getting hurt. The Unrivaled were afraid that the same kind of thing could happen to their visitors.

Andrew was certain that once the Unrivaled got to know him and his friends, everything would be different.

The Unrivaled's daily life consisted of endless rituals and ceremonies honoring one great house or another. In many ways, these events were very similar to the celebrations the Dinotopians loved so much. Except that the Unrivaled bound their ceremonies with strict rules of conduct.

For example, Andrew learned that one could easily offend a singer at an official ceremony by not singing along. Talking during an Endowment of Honor was thought to bring bad luck upon that warrior and his descendants. And disturbing a young warrior-in-training could cause him to hurt himself or another!

But, overall, the city was splendid and the people very friendly.

After two more days, Andrew was told that Lord Botolf wanted to meet him. That evening, Arri ushered him upstairs and took him through a large, beautifully carved wooden door. The knight's chamber itself was decorated with images of wolves. Statues, pedestals, columns, walls, floors, and ceilings all were painted or engraved with faded pictures of the creature.

As Andrew studied the lavish decorations, he heard a door open behind him. Andrew turned to finally meet Lord Botolf.

He gasped at what he saw.

CHAPTER 14

Lord Botolf was immense!

Obesity was not usually an issue with Saurians, but Botolf was undeniably portly. The huge Troodon came through the door and settled himself on a stone throne with wolves' heads carved into the armrests. He tapped on one of them with his claws. Around Lord Botolf's large girth was tied a forest-green sash.

Andrew lifted his eyes and met Botolf's gaze. Immediately, the knight bounded down from his throne and landed before Andrew with a thud.

"So you're the new boy, is that right?" Botolf roared.

"Yes," Andrew said quickly, eyes wide with surprise.

"And how do you feel about the great honor that's been thrust upon you?"

Andrew thought for a moment. "Undeserving," he said.

Botolf laughed. "Undeserving of being made a page to a laughingstock. Is that what you mean?"

Andrew was confused. "Lord Botolf?"

Botolf looked at Arri. "You did tell him that the House of Botolf is considered a joke, didn't you? Now that Lucius has gained more status than I have?"

Arri stared straight ahead. "I do not consider this house to be any less honorable or important."

"Fah!" said Botolf. He turned and wearily sat down on his throne again.

Andrew understood. Botolf's house had once been considered powerful, but somehow that power had been lessened. "I meant no offense," Andrew said. "Really."

Botolf sighed and looked at Andrew again. "You'll find it's not so bad here. My needs are few compared to those of my fellows." The Troodon patted his enormous belly. "As you can see by the size of my gut, my days of glorious contests are long behind me."

Arri looked sharply at Botolf. "You're a Grandmaster!" he cried. "Armies are yours to control!"

"Imaginary armies," replied Botolf, sighing.

"I'm sorry," said Andrew. "I really don't understand."

Arri and Botolf explained the basic society of the warrior Troodons. In Halcyon, a warrior gained status through skill, strength, and intelligence. The better the warrior became at these things, the more he was rewarded with possessions and rank.

When a warrior reached a certain age and level of achievement, he became a Grandmaster. The Grandmasters waged entire battles with armies of thousands—all in their heads. They sat across from each other and described what occurred.

It reminded Andrew of a contest he'd once seen. Two chess experts sat across from each other and began to play—without a chessboard or pieces! They could picture the board and the moves of its pieces entirely in their minds.

Arri and Botolf went on to explain that the Unrivaled respect skill and strategy above all else—save compassion for their fellow creatures and harmony with their surroundings.

Botolf laughed. "Do you know that for the first time in a century, the rules of the obstacle course are being changed? And it's all because of you!"

"Me?" asked Andrew, amazed.

"That's right," said Arri. "So far, three of our warriors have used your—um—*direct* route through the obstacle course to win. So the rules are being made more detailed to keep this from happening."

"But it won't help," said Botolf. "In other competitions also, our warriors are winning by doing what's now called 'pulling an Andrew.'"

Andrew broke out laughing. He couldn't believe it. He was *famous* here!

"I thought so many Troodons were staring at me because I'm human," said Andrew.

"There is that, too," said Botolf. "But in one daring act you accomplished a great deal. You brought about change. That rarely happens here. Bravo!"

Andrew smiled. So this must be how it is for Ned all the time, he thought. *I could get used to this.*

It turned out that Botolf had only one major rival—the Troodon knight and Grandmaster Lucius. Botolf's recent losses to Lucius had left him saddened.

Trying to cheer up Lord Botolf, Andrew said, "It really is an honor to be here. I meant that when I said it earlier."

"Fah!" Botolf said, waving his hand dismissively. "I'm fat and lazy. And old."

"You don't look old to me," Andrew said.

"And what would you know about it?" Suddenly Botolf leaned forward and said, "Always speak your mind in my presence, boy. But don't take that liberty when others are around."

Andrew bowed.

Botolf leaned back and sighed. "I suppose you have more questions?"

"Your people are so peaceful at heart," said Andrew. "They love and respect life."

"True."

"Then how did you ever become warriors?"

Botolf shrugged. "You sound uneasy when you use the word *warrior.* To us, it is the ultimate honor."

"I didn't mean to offend," Andrew said.

"You don't," said Botolf. "At one time there was a need for warriors on this island. That time passed. Others laid down their weapons. We found a new home and remained true to our beliefs."

"How long have you been here?"

Botolf was silent. "Does it matter? We are here. We believe what we believe."

"Yes, but—"

The Troodon knight looked sharply at Andrew. "I can't help but notice the way you keep looking at my sword. Does the sight of weapons upset you?"

"Not as much as it did when I first got here," Andrew said.

Botolf drew his sword and held it out carefully for Andrew to see. The boy was stunned at the artistry that had gone into the sword's creation. Tiny images and symbols were etched into the surface of the blade. The sword was old, with many nicks and grooves, but perfectly polished and preserved.

"This is a sword," Botolf said. "It has a cutting edge. Unless I'm mistaken, you believe a warrior uses it to hurt his opponent. To take his life, even. Correct?"

Andrew nodded. What could he say?

"I'm well aware of the Dinotopian credo 'Weapons are enemies, even to their owners.' It may surprise you to know that I agree with it."

The boy was not only surprised that Botolf agreed with the saying, but also that the knight had heard of it. The Unrivaled knew a lot about the outside world. Of course, the saying Botolf had quoted was ancient. Basic truths were seldom forgotten. The Troodons could have heard the saying long ago, before they had come to Halcyon.

"If you agree with our beliefs, why do you carry a weapon?" Andrew asked. "My father was a soldier in the British navy. He says no weapon is ever made unless someone intends to use it."

"We do use our weapons," Botolf said. "As symbols. As reminders that we must always be on guard. Look—"

Lord Botolf gestured. Arri picked up a rolled blanket. He laid it at Andrew's feet and unrolled it. Inside was a collection of farm tools, kitchen gear, and other instruments.

"There," Lord Botolf said, pointing to a scythe. "A blade as long as your arm, with an edge as sharp as any sword in the city."

"We use those for cutting grass," Andrew said.

"Of course. You wouldn't dream of using one against another living being."

"Certainly not," said Andrew.

Botolf pointed again. "And there's a cleaver. Beside it, another long blade."

Andrew nodded. "For cutting vegetables."

"Quite so," Botolf said. "But if they were not handled carefully—"

"Well, accidents happen."

"But they are to be avoided, yes?"

"Uh-huh."

Botolf pointed at two other items. "The hammer

and chisel are meant for the artisan, the sculptor, the builder. But they could be used to hurt someone as easily as the sword."

"But they're tools," Andrew said.

"Indeed," said Botolf. "You use them to create. You build things. And you do not destroy. It is the same with us. Our swords are our tools. And with them, we create our art. It is the expression of our spirits."

Andrew nodded. "I think I understand," he said. "But you'd still never convince me to pick up a sword."

"I wouldn't want to!" said Botolf. "A warrior must freely choose the sword. And that choice means a hard life of discipline and training."

Andrew shook his head. "Can't you just use sticks?"

"A blow with a stick could rob someone of his life as easily as a sword."

"True, but a stick won't cut a person."

Botolf nodded. "All right. Let's say we replaced all our swords with sticks. Warriors know they don't have to be as careful, so they begin to get lazy. More and more frequently, warriors get struck with sticks. Over time, they become used to it. Soon warriors are hitting each other with sticks on purpose. Then with fists. Then claws. Eventually you end up with blades again, but blades used in a deadly way. By using swords, as our ancestors did, we begin at that final stage. A warrior has no choice but to be careful. Accidents would have tragic consequences and are not allowed.

"More than that," Botolf continued, "the presence of such weapons reminds us to be respectful not only of the sword but also of the common blade, the scythe, the hammer, the chisel. Our swords teach us to take responsibility for every aspect of our lives. In that regard, the citizens of Halcyon and the citizens of the Realms Without are the same."

Andrew nodded. It was different and strange, but it made sense. Then a thought occurred to him. "But you're placing an awful lot of responsibility on each warrior. How are you sure each is ready?"

"A good question," Botolf said. "Only those who have trained for most of their lives are allowed to freely handle a sword. Such weapons are never drawn in anger. They are never used to settle a dispute. Such acts would be barbaric, and we, my young friend, are civilized."

Later that day, Andrew and Arri were sent to the river running beneath the city. Lord Botolf had a craving for a rare fish, and they had been sent to catch one. They were told to keep at it, even if it meant standing waist-deep in the water with nets all day.

"Where do these waters lead?" Andrew asked.

"To a well, deep under ground," Arri said. He seemed distracted.

Andrew gave him a funny look. "Why don't I be-lieve you?"

"I don't know," Arri said. "Perhaps you still haven't mastered our language."

Andrew thought for a moment. "It's a way out, isn't it?" he asked.

Arri hesitated. "Yes it is," he said. "But a very dan-gerous one. The Kraken lives in the waters beyond."

"The Kraken?" Andrew asked. Suddenly, he re-membered the painting he'd seen days earlier. "You mean the creature with the tentacles?"

Andrew saw a fish swimming near. He waded a little deeper into the waters and cast his net. "I've got one. I've got one!"

Arri looked over, then shook his head. "Wrong fish."

Sighing, Andrew let the fish go.

"The Kraken is a destroyer of many lands," Arri said. "That is what I was taught. It is rumored that the Kraken dragged the city of Poseidos to the murky depths."

"Poseidos? That's just a myth."

"To some. But the Kraken is no myth."

"How do you know?" Andrew asked. "Have you seen it?"

Arri gave a short laugh. "To look upon the Kraken is to see your own demise," he said. "That is what I was taught. Those who try to leave Halcyon by the waters will meet the Kraken. If they anger him, he will show his displeasure by finishing the job he started when he attacked this city the first time."

The Troodons do not believe that an earthquake devastated the lost city, Andrew realized. They honestly think it was this beast!

The thirteen-year-old decided to let that subject go for the moment. "So what's going on between Lucius and Lord Botolf? What started this rivalry between them?"

Arri cast his net. "Lucius is the youngest of our kind ever to achieve the title of Grandmaster. He is ruthless and has never faced defeat. While his skill cannot be argued with, his beliefs are—" Arri struggled to control his emotions. "He is without honor."

"Why?" asked Andrew.

"Once a year, the Festival of Riches is held. Many competitions take place. The overall winner of the festival is awarded the highest honor in our society, the title of Sage. The first thing the new Sage does is give away all his worldly possessions."

"Really?" asked Andrew. "You mean Botolf would lose his house?"

"Not lose it. He would give it away. Gladly. He would have the honor and pleasure of starting his life over again from the very beginning. All new challenges and adventures."

"But where would he live?" asked Andrew.

"Someone would take him in. Someone who needs help or advice. Then someone else, then another. Our people would listen to his every word and act upon it."

"What about Lucius?"

"Lord Botolf fears that if Lucius takes the prize, he will unbalance all the old traditions. He'll *keep* his wealth. He will rule our city from his throne and do away with the festival so that no one can ever take his power. He's said as much. Worse, he has support from many of the important houses."

"That does sound pretty scary," Andrew said.

Arri nodded. "Lord Botolf says that power belongs in the hands of those who wield it wisely. A lifetime of service to the Art usually ensures the necessary wisdom. But in this case—"

"So maybe Lord Botolf should fight this Lucius!" said Andrew.

Arri tapped the side of his head. "Here is where the battle will take place. It's all about confidence and belief. Lord Botolf has lost his confidence. He wonders if the battle is even worth fighting, as he sees no chance to win."

Andrew shook his head. He would need time to think about this. Then he asked Arri a question that had been on his mind for some time. "Arri, I know it was you outside the city that night in the storm. You're the one I returned the armlet to. Why did you leave?"

Arri seemed stricken. "I wasn't sure you recognized me. I hope you won't tell others. They wouldn't understand."

"No," Andrew said with a smile. "I won't tell. I think you're curious. You want to know what's out there."

"I already know," Arri said smugly.

"Oh, yeah?" Andrew asked. "What's out there then?"

The Troodon leaned over and poked Andrew's side. "Soft."

"Hey!" Andrew cried. "Stop that!"

The Troodon poked him again. "Pinklings!"

"Arri!"

"Soft pinklings, soft pinklings!"

Andrew was losing his balance. "Tickles!"

"Sofffft pinnnkklllinnngs!"

"Hey!" Andrew cried as he fell into the water, and Arri playfully cast his net over the boy.

The next day, Andrew was again summoned before Lord Botolf. A troupe of traditional dancers was performing for all the houses and would soon arrive at the House of Botolf. As Andrew waited, he asked the Troodon knight, "Do you know what I do in the world outside?"

"No, I don't," Lord Botolf said.

"I'm a keeper of stories," said Andrew. "True stories. Like the one I know about the Kraken."

Botolf roared, "The Kraken is not a subject to be taken lightly!"

"Certainly not," Andrew said. "But what you don't

know is that the beast is missing a tentacle. And I know how it happened. I heard it from the lips of someone who was there."

"Ridiculous," Botolf scoffed. "No one sees the Kraken and lives."

"Then how did your artists know what it looks like? How do you even know it exists?"

Botolf considered this. Slowly, he said, "You know one who survived an attack of the Kraken?"

"I've met him."

"So it's a human."

"I didn't say that. I said it's a him; that's all I said."

Botolf studied the boy with deep interest. "Tell me this story of yours."

"If you wish," Andrew said.

"Is it a tale of danger?"

"It is."

"Is it brief?" the Troodon asked, clearly hoping that it was not.

"No, Lord. It may consume many nights in the telling."

Botolf settled into his throne and said, "Then you'd better get started."

CHAPTER 15

Lian wondered why the Unrivaled had never renamed Halcyon. If the task were given to her, she knew what she would call it: Valhalla, the warrior's paradise!

She had been here for close to a week. Though she missed Henna, Andrew, and Ned, she was thrilled to be with the Unrivaled. During her first few days she'd learned how to communicate with them and how to behave in their public places.

Her companion was Na'dra, a swordmaster and a warrior—and a female! Lian had been sent to the House of Lucius, the Lion Herald, a Grandmaster Warrior Knight of the Sixth Order. The very idea of the lions came from the outside world. It had been carried by a human guest more than two centuries earlier.

As soon as she'd arrived, Lian had learned about the important festival coming up. It would settle once and for all the dispute over who was the greater warrior, her own Lord Lucius or "Flopbottom" Botolf, as Lucius had nicknamed him.

In a way, Lian felt sorry for old Botolf. But what

did he need with yet another victory? That warrior's glory days were long past. Lucius was young and strong! In many ways, he reminded Lian of her brothers and father in China, warriors all.

Lucius had sat with Lian, imparting his beliefs. "As a warrior, you should be strong and brave," he'd said. "Single-minded. Do not look backward or to the side when facing an enemy. Go straight forward to crush him!"

Lian was thinking of her own situation. She desperately wanted to become a warrior, but felt that the chances were slim. "What if you're up against impossible odds?" she asked.

"Don't let yourself be overcome by any task," Lucius counseled. "Even one that seems impossible. True warriors live by the belief that if they are cornered by their enemies, they will stand alone and fight. Remember, never surrender!"

Taking Lucius's words as encouragement, Lian had performed several demonstrations of her skill and training as a warrior. Lucius would not allow her to pick up a sword, and so she'd used a broom handle. The Troodon knight had applauded when she finished, but he was not impressed enough to grant her a sword.

"I don't understand," Lian said later to her friend Na'dra. They were in an open courtyard, with a clear view of the deep blue sky above. "What am I doing wrong?"

"It's not a matter of right or wrong," said Na'dra. "Your techniques are easily countered. And your attack reveals that you have something to prove. You are not at peace with yourself. You cannot hope to fight an enemy successfully when you are at war with yourself."

Lian frowned. "Show me your way, then."

"Very well," Na'dra said, drawing her sword and beginning a series of movements. When she'd finished, she said, "You see? I'll explain it to you exactly the way I was taught. Some believe that when you're pushed, you should pull back, when pulled, push forward. Instead, try this: when pushed, pivot and go around, when pulled, enter when circling. You see? It makes you one with whoever's attacking you. You go right into the attack."

Lian copied Na'dra's movements.

"My teacher explained that you want your movements to be just like the universe, always circling and swirling. You bring your enemy into this spinning circle, where you challenge and defeat his sense of balance."

Next, Na'dra took a fan from her belt and opened it. "This is made from paper," she said. "If you toss a stone at it, what happens?"

"The stone would rip it apart," Lian said immediately. "The stone is heavier. It has power."

Na'dra spun the fan until it was a blur of motion. "Watch. Toss a stone at the fan."

Lian did. She watched as Na'dra moved swiftly, allowing the stone to be swept up by the motions of the fan.

"It's captured, then tossed out," Lian observed. "You created a funnel."

Na'dra nodded. "Exactly. Now look at the fan."

"Unharmed."

"And where is the stone?"

Lian looked to one side. "Lying on the ground."

Na'dra closed the fan and tucked it back in her belt. "The enemy is defeated by its own aggression. A weapon made of something as weak as paper turns out to be more effective than one made of stone."

Lian shook her head in wonder. "I've never seen a form of fighting quite like yours."

"You've never come here before," said Na'dra. "Now, you must understand: With this technique, one defends not only herself but also her attacker. My teacher said that true victory is not in defeating an enemy. It is in making your enemy seek peace. Without enlightenment these techniques won't do you any good."

"Did Lord Lucius teach you this?" Lian asked.

Na'dra turned away. "Lord Lucius is concerned only with winning." She looked up at the cloudless sky. "Have you ever wondered what it's like to fly?"

"I rode a Skybax once."

Na'dra's eyes lit up. "Really?"

Lian told her what it was like. Na'dra listened intently, then looked at the sky once more. She seemed to be considering something. Finally, the warrior led Lian to one of the highest towers in Halcyon. They climbed a circular stone staircase and emerged on the roof. There, a large sheet covered several odd-looking items.

"What's all this?" asked Lian.

"The only way I know of flying," said Na'dra. She pulled back the sheet and revealed a wondrous collection of brightly colored kites!

Lian saw two kites shaped like butterflies. One had rich shades of blue, lavender, and gold. The other was black and orange with crimson highlights. Something that looked like clouds with tiny suns buried in them radiated from the bodies of both butterflies. Stunning patterns like stained glass completed the wings.

Other kites were ornately painted with images of warrior Troodons. One was designed to look like a glittering array of gold and silver swords. Lian saw fish swimming in a deep blue ocean on one kite, blue and red birds sailing across the sky on another.

"You made all these?" asked Lian.

"Why?" asked Na'dra unsteadily. "Don't you like them?"

Lian laughed. "I think they're amazing!"

Na'dra sighed in relief. "I fly them only at night."

"You don't share these with others?" Lian asked.

"Oh, I want to!" said Na'dra. "One of the events in the festival is the Celebration of Design. Some entries will be sculptures, others paintings. This would be my contribution."

"What made you change your mind?" asked Lian.

"Lord Lucius," said Na'dra. "He says that being gentle is the same as being weak. That expressing oneself with anything other than a sword is wrong."

"Ridiculous!"

Na'dra lowered her head. "What can I do? I'm pledged to his service."

"So you have to carry on in secret?"

"Yes."

Lian frowned. "Tell me something. How do you fly one of these?"

Na'dra's eyes grew bright once more. "You really want to know?"

"Please."

Na'dra explained that judging the direction and strength of the wind was very important. Today, for example, the winds were all around them, pushing upward.

"Below, it would be very difficult to fly," said Na'dra. "In the city, the winds are trapped. They sail this way and that, trying to escape."

Lian lifted up one of the butterflies. She could already feel the wind filling the kite, trying to take hold.

"You have to have a firm grasp on the pull line before letting go," said Na'dra.

"This cord?" asked Lian. Na'dra nodded, and Lian wrapped the cord around her arm. "Then what?"

"Push as hard as you can into the direction of the wind and let it go."

Suddenly, Lian turned and did just that!

"Wait!" cried Na'dra, but it was too late. The kite rose swiftly into the air.

Lian pulled the line taut. The wind allowed the butterfly to gently glide across the sky.

"You shouldn't have done that," Na'dra said helplessly.

Then, from the streets below, came a cheering. Na'dra looked over the edge of the roof to see a small crowd staring up at her kite.

"I doubt that Lucius will be able to object now," Lian said.

With a look of fierce determination, Na'dra launched the kite of swords and flew it beside the butterfly. The cheers of the crowd grew louder. More Troodons flooded into the street, pointing up at the kites. Warriors came out and raised their swords in tribute.

Na'dra had no idea what the consequences of this act might be. All she knew was that for this brief, soaring moment, she felt happy....

CHAPTER 16

Ned was staying with the metalsmith Silverclaw when word arrived of Lian and Na'dra's kite display.

Lord Lucius took all the credit for Na'dra's stunning work. He promised that it was only a glimpse of the grand offering Na'dra would make at the Festival of Riches.

Meanwhile, Lian was immediately moved to the House of Botolf. She wasn't sure if it was a punishment or not, but she was happy to see Andrew again.

The next day, Ned paid a visit with his Troodon host, Silverclaw. The metalsmith had come to the House of Botolf to mend armor, and Ned came along to see Andrew and Lian. Overjoyed to see each other again, the three sat in Andrew's quarters beneath the house to exchange stories.

Ned filled them in on what had happened to him since they'd been separated. At first, Ned had thought he'd been sent to the metalsmith as a punishment for losing the obstacle course event. But he quickly became fascinated by Silverclaw's amazing ability to work metal.

"Why is he called Silverclaw?" asked Andrew.

"I suppose it's because he always wears a metal glove on one hand," Ned said. "A gauntlet, he calls it."

Ned soon discovered that serving the metalsmith was a highly sought-after position. The Troodons considered making armor and weaponry both an art and a science.

"I think the Unrivaled wanted me to learn patience," said Ned. "I wasn't a very good loser when Arri beat me through the obstacle course. A part of me was stunned that I could ever lose. But it turned out for the best. I wouldn't want to be with a warrior now. Silverclaw is a friend."

Ned explained that Silverclaw was a master of his craft, the greatest armorer in Halcyon. He had five apprentices, some of whom quickly became jealous of Ned.

The apprentices had to work hard to earn their food, a place to live, and an occasional glimpse into Silverclaw's craft. As an honored human visitor, Ned alone was allowed to watch over the metalsmith's shoulder, to see Silverclaw's sketches and designs for new armors.

Ned learned the two primary techniques for making chain mail—using pliers to join links, or the more standard rivets. He also learned Silverclaw's favorite technique for making his customers happy.

Silverclaw had told Ned, "Always tell the customer that a job will take four times as long as you actually think it will. That way, even if you end up taking twice as long as you expected, the customer will think you're doing him a favor!"

"That sounds a little sneaky," Ned had said.

"Not at all!" Silverclaw had insisted. "Sometimes when warriors earn status, they become demanding and forget the value of patience. No one is above learning a good lesson."

At night Ned and Silverclaw would speak for long hours. The metalsmith loved hearing stories about Ned's childhood in Louisiana and the shipwreck that had brought him to Dinotopia. He was also fascinated by details about Dinotopian society outside the lost city.

When Ned had become aware of the other apprentices' resentment for him, he went to Silverclaw and asked for some chores. Before long, Ned was working harder than the apprentices! At one point, they came to him as a group and asked him to slow down.

But Ned had found that he couldn't stop. Being Silverclaw's prime helper and friend was too important to him. Ned pushed himself harder and harder, until one day he collapsed from exhaustion.

The apprentices later explained to Ned that they weren't being lazy; they were pacing themselves. Creating armor and weapons was a grueling process. Ned had promised to heed their advice and slow down.

Silverclaw had come to visit Ned as he rested. The metalsmith asked why Ned had pushed himself beyond his limits.

"I wanted to make you happy," Ned told him. "I wanted to impress you."

Ned explained that all his life, things had come easily to him. But here there was no guarantee that he would succeed. For once, he wanted to work hard for something.

Silverclaw had sighed heavily. The Troodon held up his left claw, the one always covered by a metal glove. "Do you see this?"

"Your claw?"

"I wear this gauntlet because of an accident I had when I was much younger. I was like you, so anxious to please. I was given my first major task to complete on my own: designing the armor for a fast-rising young warrior named Botolf. I got the job because I said I could get it done more quickly and better than any of my teacher's other pupils. Then one night, tragedy struck. I wasn't resting. I was pushing myself to the limits of my endurance and beyond."

Ned had watched nervously as the Troodon began to remove his silver glove.

"This happened," Silverclaw said.

The glove came off. Ned gasped, expecting to see something deformed and twisted. Instead, the claw was perfectly normal.

"I don't understand," said Ned.

"I tripped and almost plunged my claw into a vat of molten metal. Fortunately, my teacher was in the room, watching me. I had no idea. He rescued me."

"So why do you wear the gauntlet?"

"To remind me of what my foolishness and my pride nearly cost me. My teacher volunteered to help with the armor in secret—on the condition that I wear this gauntlet for the rest of my life. Since then I have looked at it often and realized that there are no shortcuts in life. None without dire cost. Any job worth doing is worth doing well. And whatever time and effort it takes—so be it," Silverclaw had said.

Ned sat back, his story at an end. That's when Andrew spoke up. "You know, that's kind of what's happening with Lord Lucius. Lucius wants *shortcuts,* just as Silverclaw did. The thing is, it won't be Lucius who'll suffer if he wins the festival. It'll be all the Unrivaled. I think we should see if there's some way we can help Lord Botolf—"

Lian sprang from her chair. "Andrew! That's unfair! You want to condemn Lord Lucius, but you haven't talked to him! You don't know what he really believes!"

Andrew said, "But according to Lord Botolf, Lucius has publicly stated—"

"No!" said Lian. "I've spoken with Lord Lucius. I know how easily he could be misunderstood. He believes what my uncle and my father believe—that a

warrior without an enemy, without a cause, is no warrior at all!"

She went to the stairs.

"Lian, wait—" Andrew called.

"No," she said, storming up the stairs. "I'm going
to see if Lord Lucius will take me back. And if he will,
I intend to try to help him win the festival."

With that she left, slamming the door behind her.

Andrew and Ned stared at each other in silence.

Finally, Ned said, "Do you think maybe we're
wrong about Lucius?"

"I don't know," said Andrew. "I just hope he
doesn't disappoint Lian. I really hope he doesn't...."

CHAPTER 17

The day of the festival had arrived!

The warriors of the Unrivaled and their families gathered in the coliseum, where the various competitions would be staged.

Lian had been welcomed back by Lucius. Andrew and Ned had tried to visit her, but she'd refused to see them. Na'dra had told them, "When the festival is over, she'll see you. Now she is working very hard to prepare and doesn't wish to be disturbed. I'm sorry. Breathe deep, seek peace."

Andrew and Ned had gone to Lord Botolf and asked to enter the festival. The Troodon knight had refused to allow them to compete. But he could see uses for them, especially Andrew. So, Botolf had Andrew and Ned trained to work as pages. They would assist the knights.

Soon the two friends had learned the names and functions of the various pieces of a suit of armor. They understood that a poleyn was a knee protector and that a greave covered the lower leg. They were taught that a chain-mail frock called an arming doublet always went on first. The arming doublet contained waxed points for attaching other pieces of armor. The significance of breastplates and the knights' various colored sashes quickly became second nature to them. It turned out that the brightest colors denoted the highest rank, the dullest, the lowest.

On festival day, Lord Botolf arrived at the coliseum wearing Silverclaw's latest suit of armor and a brand-new sword. His rival, Lord Lucius, wore the armor and sword of his ancestors.

Botolf took Andrew to one side. The portly Troodon knight seemed happier than he had been in days.

"Tonight you're going to tell me how the Kraken's story ends," said Botolf firmly.

"Of course I will," Andrew said. "Right after the celebration of your victory."

Botolf waved his claw as if to dismiss such talk, but the possibility of winning clearly delighted him.

The knight was called away, and Arri approached Andrew.

"I don't know what you did," said Arri. "But I can't remember a time when Lord Botolf seemed so free of worries."

Andrew shrugged. "My stories took his mind off things, that's all. Gave him something else to think about."

A horn was sounded. The first rounds of competition would soon begin. A trio of Troodons wearing golden armor entered the arena, and a hush fell upon the crowd.

The warrior in the middle stepped forward and said, "By practicing our art every day, we gain strength. By learning from our mistakes, we gain wisdom. By crossing swords with an opponent, we gain power."

The Troodon on the left joined his friend and said, "To the fine warriors who will compete this day I say this: Fix your minds on the four oaths and put selfishness behind you. Win or lose, you cannot fail."

The last of the golden-armored Troodons came forward and said, "These are the four oaths. Follow the way of the warrior. Be useful to our cause. Be respectful to others. Exist for the good of all."

Without another word, the three Troodons turned and left the arena. Another horn sounded, and six pairs of warriors, swords drawn, took up positions on the "battlefield." Arri was one of the warriors. His sash was forest green, the color for Lord Botolf's House. Two other warriors with green sashes were among the fighters too. They were facing warriors with pale yellow sashes.

Andrew and Ned watched the Unrivaled's finest warriors engage in one Flourish—or personal competition—at a time. The warriors moved with blinding speed. Their weapons crashed together. Fierce battle cries sounded. The moment a warrior's defenses faltered and the opponent had a clear opening, the Flourish was brought to a halt and a winner declared.

Two of Lord Botolf's three warriors won their competitions. Three warriors with red sashes also won. They were from the House of Lord Lucius.

Arri's Flourish was the last to be staged. As Arri faced his opponent, one of Lord Botolf's other warriors said, "Remember to do what the Andrew said!"

Arri nodded and gave a slight laugh. He looked straight into the eyes of his opponent. The other warrior seemed nervous.

"What did he say to do?" asked the other warrior.

"That would be telling," Arri said.

The signal came, and their Flourish began. Arri faced his opponent bravely and very quickly triumphed!

At the outskirts of the arena, Grizzardle ambled over to Andrew and Ned. "Lord Botolf's warriors have done well. As have Lord Lucius's warriors."

"The warriors with the red sashes?" asked Andrew.

"Indeed." The Bagaceratops chuckled. "Everyone's talking about you. They want to know how 'the Andrew' is going to help Lord Botolf win."

"I'm just standing here," said Andrew. "I'm not doing anything."

"From the look of things," said Grizzardle, "that might be enough."

Andrew nodded. He and Lord Botolf had talked about the importance of strategy in any conflict. Just *knowing* that Andrew was "helping" Lord Botolf gave the older knight and his warriors an edge.

The young storyteller also had a few other surprises in mind, which would come into play later in the festival.

There were several more rounds of Flourishes after Arri's. In some, one warrior faced two opponents. In others, as many as six warriors from one house faced an equal number of opponents from a rival house.

Not all the events in the festival centered around battle. Many involved reading poetry or displaying artwork. The clowns appeared to amuse the audience. Games were played, including a chess match with living pieces. The warriors representing pieces replaced their colored sashes with either white or black sashes. The strategists in charge of each side were previous winners of the festival.

Na'dra won the Celebration of Design by flying a kite that looked like a dragon. Several other houses had attempted to create kites too. But their kites were poor imitations of Na'dra's creative masterpieces.

The day wore on. Soon the warriors facing Lord Botolf's men stopped worrying about Andrew. Many competitions had been won and lost, and so far nothing unusual had occurred. The warriors from the other houses decided that Andrew and Ned were simply serving as pages, nothing more. Of course, that was exactly what Andrew wanted them to think.

As midday approached, a massive feast was laid

out on the field. Andrew and Ned marveled at the array of fruits, vegetables, and fish. All were specially prepared with recipes handed down from generation to generation. Arri and Grizzardle ate with Lord Botolf and his two pages.

"Has anyone seen Lian?" Andrew asked.

Grizzardle said, "I know that she's been entered in the Shadow Dance. But I haven't seen her."

The Shadow Dance was a competition for beginning warriors. It was scheduled to begin just after lunch.

"I'm worried about her," Ned said.

Andrew nodded. "Me too."

Before long, the feast came to an end. The tables were cleared away, and the young warriors participating in the Shadow Dance appeared. Andrew was startled to see that Lian had been given a sword!

A large marble slab had been placed at the center of the arena. Lian stood at one end of the marble slab, positioned so that her shadow was directly behind her. Another fledgling warrior stood six feet before her. Judges stood at either side of Lian, far enough away to avoid the reach of her sword. The warrior standing before Lian turned her back to the young woman. The warrior's shadow stretched out behind her. When Lian looked down, it was as if she were facing an opponent made of shadows.

The beginning warriors of the Shadow Dance were too inexperienced to actually cross swords with one another. They could not be trusted to pull back in time. If one accidentally harmed another, even in the least way, he or she would be subjected to the Great Silence. The Shadow Dance allowed new warriors to compete in the festival with no risk of injury.

Lian raised her weapon, preparing to battle her opponent's shadow, when Na'dra came forward.

"I must speak with my friend," Lian said.

The judges indicated that this was acceptable. Lian stepped off the marble slab to talk to Na'dra.

"What's wrong?" asked Lian.

"It's Lord Lucius," said Na'dra. "He directs you to lose this contest."

"What?"

Na'dra looked pained. "I'm sorry. It's the message he told me to pass on to you."

"I don't believe you."

The Troodon was stunned. "I'm your friend. I wouldn't lie to you."

"Do you want me to fail?"

"My wishes don't matter. I'm sworn to Lord Lucius's service. I delivered the Floating Dragon and won a competition in his name."

"Then you've got another reason."

"Lian—"

"No!" Lian said. She went back to her place on the marble slab. Na'dra turned and left.

From the far side of the arena, Andrew watched as the signal was given and "combat" began.

Lian's opponent spun her sword over her head and brought her blade down in sharp, quick movements.

Several feet behind the Troodon, well out of harm's way, Lian met the shadow's attack. All she could do was counter the unpredictable movements of her opponent. To win this competition, Lian would have to meet 100 shadow "blows" without once faltering. Then she would trade places with her opponent and do it all over again.

To those in the audience, it looked as if Lian and the Troodon warrior were moving as one. It was a strange but beautiful dance.

Lian used the techniques Na'dra had taught her. She focused entirely on the shadow and her own breathing. There was no outside world as she wove elegant patterns through the air with her sword. This was the moment she had dreamed of all her life: to be accepted as a warrior. Na'dra's terrible demand that she do less than her best was insulting, but Lian did not even think of it now. She would not be distracted.

Suddenly, the competition was called to a halt by the judges. Lian couldn't believe it. She had won the first part of the competition!

She glanced around and saw Lord Lucius staring at her. He nodded in her direction. She bowed in return.

Lian and her opponent switched places and readied themselves. This time, Lian would be the attacker. The signal was given, and Lian leaped into a series of moves with her sword.

She began with the traditional forms of Troodon swordplay. Then, once Lian was certain that her opponent had been lured into a false sense of security, she changed her style. One moment she was thrusting predictably with her sword. The next, she was moving in ways that her uncle had taught her, ways that no Troodon except Na'dra had seen before!

Suddenly, Lian heard an oath behind her. In the next moment, the competition was over. Turning, Lian watched her opponent lay her sword at Lian's feet.

She had won!

The audience exploded with cheers. Lian raised her sword, basking in the victory. She saw Andrew and Ned. Although they were on Lord Botolf's side, they were cheering Lian along with everyone else. Lian felt bad about the way she had spoken to them before and vowed to make it up to them later.

After her win, a Troodon led Lian to a darkened corridor. Lord Lucius was waiting for her there. The Troodon knight gestured impatiently, and the warrior who had brought Lian turned and left.

Once they were alone, Lucius hissed, "How dare you gain victory!"

"But—I was fighting for your glory," Lian said, confused.

"Then it is Na'dra's fault," Lucius said. "She didn't give you my message."

Lian went pale. "Then it's true? You really sent that message?"

"Of course. Why would you question such a thing?"

"Because Na'dra had shown her disloyalty. I thought she wanted to help Botolf win."

"Her disloyalty? Didn't you see her Floating Dragon?"

Lian said, "Yes, but—"

"So you would have honored my wishes," Lucius said. "You thought Na'dra was betraying me. I should have talked to you myself. Perhaps there is hope for you yet."

"I don't understand," Lian said, stunned by this turn of events. "Why would you want me to fail?"

"Because you're Botolf's!" Lucius hissed.

Lian's jaw dropped. "No, I'm—"

"In spirit you are weak like him. Everyone knows that I took you back in just to shame him. To show that his beliefs are foolish. That his strengths are illusions."

"But Lord Lucius," Lian said, "I've always been taught that doing anything less than your best is wrong. How could you expect me to do such a thing? It's without honor!"

"Honor!" Lucius spat. "You asked to be thought of as a warrior!"

"Yes," said Lian. "I did."

"In battle, warriors are often asked to sacrifice themselves for the greater glory of their masters. Your honor means nothing. You pledged to serve me! To raise me up to new heights!"

Finally, Lian understood. Quietly, she said, "It's true. Everything they've been saying about you is true."

"That I will win today?" asked Lucius. "That I will keep what I win, and use my power to rule? Of course it's true. Now come with me. I must find a way to turn your victory to my advantage."

Lian stood perfectly still as the Troodon knight turned and walked away. When he realized that Lian wasn't with him, he stopped.

Without looking back, he said, "You're not following me."

"No, not anymore," Lian replied.

Lucius went on without another word.

CHAPTER 18

There were only two events left. First there was to be a competition between the most highly ranked warriors of the remaining houses. Then, finally, a mental battle would be held between the two remaining knights.

Andrew stood near the mouth of a darkened corridor leading to the arena. He smiled at Ned. Their special tactics would finally come into play in these last events.

The competition had been thinned from eleven houses to four. Botolf and Lucius were tied in the number of wins. Soon, three warriors from each of the four remaining houses would take the arena to participate in a Flourish. When this competition was over, only two houses would remain.

"Okay," Ned called. "They're ready."

Andrew raised his hand and signaled to the golden-armored officials that their warriors were ready to take the field. The warriors of the other three houses had already done so. A horn sounded to indicate the warriors' entrance. Andrew smiled, thinking about what would come next.

He watched as the solemn warriors of the other three houses entered the arena. Songs were sung to their glory. Now, nine warriors were all in their places. Only Botolf's warriors were missing.

"Now," said Andrew.

Ned looked back into the tunnel and motioned for a group of Troodons to come forward. Andrew and Ned leaned against the walls of the corridors to allow their companions room to pass.

The audience exploded in laughter as five of Silverclaw's apprentices leaped into the daylight, followed by Lord Botolf's warriors.

Lian, who stood with Na'dra, giggled at the sight.

The Saurians were dressed in bright, silly costumes that Silverclaw's apprentices had worked on for many days. One grim-faced Troodon was dressed as a half-peeled banana. Others wore the costumes of bunnies and cherries. Another was dressed as a panda bear, though the Dinotopians had only heard tales of such creatures. The last apprentice was dressed as a raging, uncoordinated Tyrannosaurus rex.

The apprentices sang a ridiculous warrior's song while marching just ahead of Botolf's trio of warriors. All three of the combatants wore armor that made them look like buck-toothed wolves!

Lucius saw Botolf, who was dressed as a large spiral timepiece, and cried, "What is the meaning of this?"

Botolf shrugged. "These competitions are meant as a celebration of life. Win or lose, we wish to have fun."

"Ridiculous!"

"Taking the miracle of life for granted is ridiculous. Not enjoying every precious moment we have is ridiculous." Botolf laughed. "Now, if you'll excuse me, these fine warriors have a competition to enter!"

Andrew smiled as he looked over at Ned. The older boy had managed to convince Silverclaw and his apprentices to create these costumes and strange sets of armor totally in secret.

The other nine warriors in the arena were stunned by the sight of their opponents.

"I can't fight that!" cried one of Lucius's warriors. "How am I supposed to keep a straight face?"

Lucius stormed over. "You'll do what you have to do!" he thundered.

The surprises didn't end there. Another of Lucius's warriors shouted, "They don't have swords! Their scabbards are empty!"

All three of Botolf's warriors, Arri included, reached down and grabbed at the empty air where their hilts would be.

"Of course we have our swords!" said Arri. "Can't you see them?"

Lucius was beside himself. He ran over to the golden-armored judges and attempted to have Botolf's warriors barred from the competition.

One of the judges sighed. "Well, there is nothing in the rules that stops the warriors from wearing funny costumes and armor."

Another judge leaned forward and said, "And swords aren't specifically mentioned, either."

"I knew they'd pull an Andrew," said another of the judges cheerfully.

Lucius stalked over to Botolf. "You're disgracing our traditions!" he said.

"I'm keeping an open mind," said Botolf. "Grandmasters fight with phantom armies. Why can't our warriors fight with phantom swords?"

"It has never been done before!"

Botolf leaned in and whispered, "And no winner of the festival has ever kept the riches for himself, either."

Lucius drew back and stared at Botolf. Then the Troodon walked off with his head raised, looking as if he'd won some kind of victory. "Fine! Let your warriors pretend to do battle. I'd like to see them find opponents willing to put up with such nonsense!"

As if in response, the soldiers of the other two houses removed their swords and handed them to their pages. They took up positions as if they were holding swords, even though their hands were empty.

Lucius looked on with disdain. Finally, he gave the order for his men to part with their swords.

"I don't believe it," Ned said as he watched from the sidelines. "They're going to go along with it!"

"I told you! I told you your idea was a good one," said Andrew.

The judges moved closer to the warriors. "Judging this is going to be challenging!" one of them said. When everyone was set, the leader of the judges ordered the warriors to begin.

For a few moments, all the warriors were thrown off by having to fight with imaginary swords. A real sword had weight. It was like an extension of their arms. But Botolf's and Lucius's warriors quickly adjusted. The six warriors from the other two houses "fell."

An instant before the warriors from the final two houses could engage, the competition was brought to a halt.

"Only two houses remain!" called one of the judges. "The House of Botolf and the House of Lucius! Will the Grandmasters please come forward for the final competition!"

Lord Botolf sighed, then turned to Andrew. "Andrew, your imagination and your belief in the impossible has made all the difference to me. I thank you."

"You've got me all wrong," said Andrew. "I don't believe in the impossible."

"You don't?"

"No. I think *anything's* possible. There's a difference."

"Anything's possible," said Botolf.

Andrew smiled. "Especially here on Dinotopia."

130

Botolf nodded. "I'll remember that."

With those words, the Troodon knight went off to face his rival.

Two large stone chairs were hauled into the center of the arena. Lord Lucius was already waiting in one of them.

Botolf sat down across from Lucius and leaned forward. The older knight asked, "Do you ever admit to anyone that you started as one of my warriors?"

"Never," said Lucius.

Botolf smiled grimly. "That's what I thought."

In this final competition, Lucius and Botolf would each command an imaginary army. Each had an equal number of warriors. The judges would award victory for each battle based on the strength of the tactics used.

The judges, all former Grandmasters, described in great detail the location of the imaginary war. The fight would take place in a dangerous mountain terrain. With that, the competition began.

At the outset, it appeared that Lucius had the advantage. He described his army surging forward boldly and was awarded one skirmish after another. Botolf attempted to set traps and ambushes, but Lucius always seemed to be one step ahead of him.

Then, when fully half of Botolf's forces had been wiped out, the older Troodon knight made a brilliant maneuver. He led both armies into a trap from which there would be no escape for either side. Lucius attempted to withdraw his forces, but it was too late. All the warriors from both armies fell a great distance into a churning river that took them out to sea. There would be no return for any of them. Only Lucius and Botolf were left.

"Now we stand at either end of a bridge," Botolf said. "It's an important bridge. Both your people and mine need it to survive."

"Our people are gone," said Lucius bitterly.

"No. The warriors are gone. Their families, their wives and children, are still with us. So are the artisans, the fishermen, and many more. They need this bridge."

"Very well."

"The one who wins this battle gains control over the bridge," Lord Botolf said. "The fate of all our people will be in that one's hands." Botolf paused and looked steadily at Lucius. "I await your decision."

With a start, Lucius realized the trap he'd been led into. He stared at his opponent in barely restrained fury.

They remained like this for several long minutes.

Several hundred yards away, Andrew turned to Arri. "What's going on?" he whispered. "I don't get it. Why did everything just stop?"

Arri explained. "It's a matter of personal honor. The next move is Lucius's, but there's really no move he can make. There are only two choices: Lucius can either step forward or step back. But both have already been determined by Botolf. To step forward is to admit that he has no control over his actions. He'd just be doing something that Botolf has already set up for him."

"Right," said Ned, standing with them. "And to step back is admitting he's afraid, and that's the same as being beaten."

Andrew nodded. "So he doesn't move, and it's a tie."

"Unless Lord Lucius can think of a way out of the trap before the judges lose patience," Arri said.

Andrew looked at the judges. They were already looking at one another impatiently.

Suddenly, Lord Lucius began to laugh. It was an eerie sound.

One of the judges said, "Do you have something to say?"

"I do," said Lucius. "The waters on either side of the bridge begin to churn. The earth itself trembles. There is a horrible roar, and the Kraken appears!"

The crowd gasped.

Lucius went on, "The creature is enraged by the sacrifice of so many fine warriors. It knows that the world is out of balance and that the balance must be restored! Its black tentacles rise up out of the water. The Kraken's single eye fixes on my opponent, Botolf, the one responsible for the sacrifice of all the warriors. It tries to reach him, but it cannot. Botolf is on the shore just before the bridge, safe from its grasp. So instead it vents its anger on the bridge, attacking it, threatening to destroy it! All this time, it sings its song of vengeance, of rage! The beast's cries sound like thunder."

Lucius smiled sweetly at Botolf. "Your move," he said.

From the sidelines, Andrew watched as Lord Botolf sat in silent contemplation. He took a quick glance in Andrew's direction, then looked away again.

Next to Andrew, Ned said, "He's got Botolf. I don't believe it!"

"It's true," said Arri. "If Lord Botolf fights the Kraken, he will not survive. No one ever has."

Andrew thought of the story he'd been telling Lord Botolf. There was a way, if only Lord Botolf could see the ending of the tale that Andrew had been saving for tonight.

Lord Botolf stared at the ground, concentrating on his options.

Lord Lucius sat back, confident and relaxed. "Judges?"

"Silence," said the first of the golden-armored Troodons. "He will have at least as much time as we granted you."

Suddenly, Lord Botolf straightened up and said, "I step onto the bridge."

"To your doom and defeat," muttered Lucius smugly.

The first judge bellowed, "Lucius, you will not be warned again!"

Lord Botolf was unfazed. "The bridge sways beneath me. I travel along the bridge until I am midway across it. I see one of the Kraken's tentacles reach for me, and I draw my sword. The tentacle wraps itself around me, and I am plucked up into the air. The creature's head leaves the waters. I see its terrible maw."

Lucius settled back in his throne. He glanced to the judges and opened his hands imploringly. Clearly, his opponent faced defeat. Why go on with this? They shook their heads.

Lord Botolf said, "There are tales in the Realms Without of humans who allowed themselves to be swallowed up by whales and found ways to escape from their bellies. But the Kraken has row after row of sharp teeth. I know that once I am between its jaws, I am done."

One of the judges said, "Lord Botolf, we implore you to stop and admit defeat."

Lucius nodded.

But the elder Troodon continued. "I listen to the Kraken's wails. They are not cries of anger. The song it sings is not one of vengeance."

Lord Lucius bolted forward in his throne. "I object to this!"

The judges told him to be silent. "In all the tales of the Kraken," one of them said, "many ideas have come forth about its song. Yours was only one way of looking at it."

"The song is one of loneliness and frustration,"

said Botolf. "The Kraken is not evil. It was not responsible for the destruction of Halcyon so long ago. All the Kraken wants is companionship—someone else to sing its song. And just before I am dragged into its maw, I begin to sing."

Lord Lucius sprang to his feet. "You can't be serious!"

Andrew smiled. Lord Botolf had figured it out. Andrew and his stories had made a difference after all!

The judges told Lucius to sit down and be quiet.

Botolf finished his tale. "The Kraken falls silent and listens to my song. It looks at me, then gently sets me back on the bridge. The creature silently disappears beneath the waters."

Lucius waited. When he was certain that Botolf was done, he said, "But you have forgotten your opponent! I charge forward and claim my victory—"

"No," said one of the judges. "To attack now is without honor. To do anything except pledge yourself to the warrior who saved the bridge is wrong."

"I will not!" cried Lucius.

Another judge shrugged. "You must. The bridge was needed to ensure the mutual survival of both peoples. He saved everyone."

"But all our warriors—"

"There will be no more argument," the first judge said. "Accept your defeat graciously, Lucius."

The warrior turned and stormed away from the competition. The crowd cheered. Lucius came over to his warriors and stopped before Lian and Na'dra.

"Come on," Lucius hissed.

No one moved.

"What's wrong with you?" Lucius asked.

Na'dra answered. "Your warriors were swept out to sea. You have none in this land."

Lucius stared at her for a moment. Then he turned away and headed out of the arena, his step a little less sure.

Lian and Na'dra joined Andrew, Ned, and Arri. Together, they greeted the winner of the festival— Lord Botolf.

"Lord Botolf, there's something I've got to ask," Andrew said as the knight embraced him.

"Anything for you," the Troodon replied.

"I think it's time for us to return to our homes," said Andrew. He looked at his friends. Ned and Lian nodded. "Our families will be missing us. Do you know of a way out?"

Lord Botolf nodded sadly. "I do know of a way, though I hesitate to tell you. I will miss you very much! But if that is what you wish, I shall help you. The way I know is sacred. I will show it to you my-self."

"I want to go with them," said Na'dra. "I want to learn to fly a Skybax, if I can."

Arri stepped forward. "And I wish to see the island and all its wonders."

Behind them, Silverclaw and his apprentices came

forward. The metalsmith said, "The Realms Without never appealed to me before. But Ned has made me curious. I want to go too."

Botolf said, "There are traditions to consider. The sword must always return to its sheath!"

Andrew smiled. "Where I'm from, they say, 'No egg rolls far from the nest.'"

Lord Botolf raised an eyebrow. "Very wise," he said.

Andrew tilted his head sideways and thought for a moment.

"Uh-oh," Ned said, looking at Andrew suspiciously. "I know what that means. We're in for a—"

"I heard a story once," said Andrew. "About an elephant and its tether."

"I've heard of elephants!" said Botolf.

Andrew noticed that the cheers of the crowd had died away. He suddenly had a much larger audience than he'd expected. He looked at Lian and Ned, who smiled encouragingly.

Taking a deep breath, Andrew said, "When elephants are young, they are often placed on tethers by humans to keep them from wandering off. They become used to having the tether. Then, when they are older, the tethers are removed—but the elephants stay where they are. They've become so used to being tied down that the tether isn't needed anymore."

"You mean they could just walk off?" asked Lord Botolf.

"They could, but they never do. They still feel bound. If you'll forgive me, I think the Unrivaled are like that. Bound by traditions. Sometimes traditions are good. But sometimes they can limit our chances to grow and to explore. Dinotopia is waiting for you to explore. The others who live on this island would welcome you—"

"Though it might be best for all if we leave our swords behind," suggested Arri with a smile.

Lord Botolf thought about this. He looked out over the residents of the lost city. "How many of you are curious about the Realms Without?" he bellowed.

At first, no one raised a hand. Then someone did, then someone else, and soon dozens had joined in.

Lord Botolf nodded. "Andrew, I'll admit you've made me curious too. Maybe in a year, when my duties as Sage are complete, I'll come looking for you."

"Or I could come back to visit," Andrew said happily.

"You would be welcome," said Lord Botolf. "All of you would be most welcome!"

CHAPTER 19

The next day Andrew, Ned, and Lian led a small group of the Unrivaled to the Dinosaur Olympics. Arri, Na'dra, Silverclaw, and several dozen residents of Halcyon were happy to meet the many Dinotopians enjoying the festivities.

The appearance of the Unrivaled created quite a stir at first. Malik greeted his fellow Troodons with astonishment and joy. He was with Bix, a Protoceratops who looked like a cross between a hog and a parrot. Bix was a highly regarded diplomat in Dinotopia.

"The Saurians of the Unrivaled are legendary among my species," Malik explained. "They were our paladins, our protectors. But then they passed into legend."

"We found a home," Na'dra explained. "One where we could refine our Art."

"Why did you poor dears hide yourselves away for so long?" asked Bix.

"We weren't hiding," said Silverclaw. "We were happy to stay in Halcyon."

"And now?" asked Malik.

"We're curious," said Arri. "Curious to see if we have anything to offer the rest of Dinotopia."

As the day went on, Arri noticed a young man who was about to enter one of the last competitions of the Olympics. The boy was very nervous.

"Breathe deep, seek peace," said Arri.

"Thanks," the boy said with a sigh. "It's Race Day, you see. I'm one of the Ring Riders. I'll be standing on the back of a Deinocheirus, rounding that track you see in the distance while trying to collect rings."

"Have you prepared for this event?"

"Yes," he said breathlessly. "But there are so many people. And I'm afraid I might disappoint someone."

Arri understood. He had felt this way in his own early days among the Unrivaled's many competitions. Arri led the boy aside and taught him the Unrivaled's ancient method of focusing the spirit. The lad quickly came to understand how to control his breathing. He also learned how to focus his attention solely on the task at hand.

"Imagine your life as a forty-room mansion," said Arri. "Each of your concerns has its own proper place. You must put each of your worries in its room and lock the door behind it. Then you must go where your heart tells you. You wish to do your best at this competition, yes? Winning or losing doesn't really matter."

"That's right."

"Then find the room in which you have trained for this event. The room where you have dreamed of being a part of the Dinosaur Olympics. Find that room and seal yourself within it until the race is over."

Soon the young man was called to the race. He was calmer now, much more focused.

And when he and his partners won, he thanked Arri before all the people and Saurians gathered for the Olympics.

"I guess we *do* have something to offer the rest of Dinotopia after all," Arri said to Andrew.

"Of course you do," said Andrew.

"And it seems the Dinotopians have something to offer us!" exclaimed Silverclaw after meeting a metalsmith from Volcaneum. They admired each other's work and promised to visit each other's workshops. Silverclaw's apprentices, who had come along, were thrilled.

Andrew and Ned were on their way to the storytelling event when Na'dra and Lian crossed in front of them.

"A garden?" Na'dra said. "But what's so special about planting a garden?"

"When we get home," Lian said, "I'll show you. Then we'll see about getting you to Skybax Camp."

Finally, the storytelling event began. Andrew was asked to go first. He was no longer worried about winning this competition. All he wanted to do was bring joy and happiness to the assembled listeners.

Just before Andrew took the stage, he was stopped by Bix.

"I have an idea," said the Protoceratops. "Do you think the Unrivaled would consider accompanying our caravans through the Rainy Basin? We could use their help."

"I think that's a great idea," said Andrew. "In fact, I'll propose it to Lord Botolf myself."

Andrew left Bix and took his place on the stage. A large crowd of humans and Saurians of every kind waited patiently for him to begin.

"So. You have stories to tell?" asked Theocritus, a squat six-foot-long Goyocephale with tiny front limbs. Theocritus had a flat head and a blue and gold hide. His eyes were dark and soulful. He was the master of ceremonies.

Andrew looked up and smiled. "I do. A story of mystery, danger, and excitement."

"I don't suppose there's anything like friendship in this tale?" Ned asked from the audience.

Andrew laughed and said, "There is. In fact, friendship is the most important thing about it."

Ned beamed at those words.

"I will begin at the beginning," said Andrew. "Our hero rides upon a wagon drawn by a friendly Pachycephalosaurus named Thumptail. When he set out, our hero had no idea how far and wide his journey would take him. All he knew was that it had been a magical day—or so he believed at the time. What he would learn soon enough was that the true magic still lay far ahead...."